Sy

of

Harmony

William N. Chiu

iUniverse books may be ordered through booksellers or by contacting:

iUniverse
1663 Liberty Drive
Bloomington, IN 47403
www.iuniverse.com
1-800-Authors (1-800-288-4677)

Because of the dynamic nature of the Internet, any Web addresses or
links contained in this book may have changed since publication and may
no longer be valid. The views expressed in this work are solely those of
the author and do not necessarily reflect the views of the publisher, and
the publisher hereby disclaims any responsibility for them.

ISBN: 978-1-4401-4876-7 (sc)
ISBN: 978-1-4401-4877-4 (ebook)

Printed in the United States of America

iUniverse rev. date: 05/20/2009

Foreword

By *Joanna LaRocca* (Fifth Grade Teacher, PS 196)

      William Chiu has written a novel that combines friendship and love despite today's all too common world of terrorism and despair. It is clear that this author incorporates both reality and fiction to create a novel which will captivate young audiences of all backgrounds. Through his writing, William demonstrates a thorough understanding of the impact of historical events on people of all ages. There is warmth in his writing, and a true connection with the main characters. Children who read this novel will not have a problem identifying with Paul, Max, Julie and Christopher. Adults may as well find themselves connected with the adults in the story. Chiu's story of love in friendship and family is further enhanced by the incorporation of other genres, such as nonfiction and poetry, as well. He supports the theme of love and caring throughout the book and in the end, the reader feels a deep hope that he will find his parents again.

I had the honor of teaching William Chiu in fourth grade and now in fifth grade. William came to my classroom as a writer, and he will be graduating from my classroom as a novelist. His novel demonstrates his passion for historical knowledge, while also incorporating his imagination of fictional characteristics as well. William takes any genre, and compliments it with another, which captivates the reader, and challenges their own prior knowledge. When William writes, he takes his readers on a journey through a world of unique characters and exciting adventures.

William's passion for learning is manifested with this story. It is my hope that all children who read this can fully appreciate what the author has done. By taking reality and giving it a spin into the fictional world, he brings the reader through an adventure. He truly helps his readers relate to the many obstacles which the characters face in this exciting adventure.

Symbol of Harmony

About the Author

William N. Chiu is a happy boy attending PS196 in Forest Hills, New York City. This is his first novel written during the summer after 4th grade in elementary school. Poetries in the book were previously written in classroom during 2nd and 4th grades.

He was born in New York City and is a big Yankee fan. He loves baseball and music. He plays baseball in the Forest Hills Little League and sings in the school chorus. He is trained in classical music. His favorite composer is Frederic

Chopin. He plays piano and has performed in recitals and concerts since the age of four, but he is very shy in speaking to a large audience.

Like many kids, he also enjoys movies, cooking, chess, travel, computer games, legos, play dates and many different sports and adventures.

Acknowledgements

I want to thank my editor, Patrick, who gave me valuable criticism and encouragement.

I also want to thank my mom who taught me how to use Microsoft Word. It is much easier to edit and revise writings on a word processor.

Finally, I must thank my good friends, Alex and Molly who helped me with the art works. The book would not be the same without their contributions and talents. They deserve all the credits in making this a beautiful book!

William Chiu

Symbol of Harmony

Summer Writing

This book is dedicated to my teacher
Ms. LaRocca,
who taught me how to write a novel in the
fourth grade,
in celebration of her wedding.

Symbol of Harmony

This story

happens in

the future...

not very far

away ...

Symbol of Harmony

Chapter 1

Walking Through the Rain

---

*C*hristopher Villson looked blankly out of the window.

There was nothing to do, nothing to think about, nothing to worry about. That was except for the first day of school. That one word spread over his thoughts. He thought about whether or not he would make any friends and hoped that his new teacher

16

would not be like his old teacher, Mr. Bruntford, who would punish the entire class if one student misbehaved.

Tomorrow will be his first day. He felt like crying. His best friends had gone away to vacation. He was going to ask his friend Harold, from last year's class, to come over, but he had forgotten that Harold had moved away.

He decided to go outside for a walk. He took his favorite umbrella. It was a Disney umbrella with all the Disney characters smiling at him. He saw Buzz, the toy super hero. They seemed so happy. Christopher felt like yelling at them to make them frown. He wanted to make them feel like the way he was feeling.

Then he shook his head. What was he thinking? He was talking to pictures on the umbrella!

He was worrying about his first day of school of seventh grade, when he already experienced this seven times including kindergarten? Not to mention preschool!

Christopher glumly sat on a fence.

With his umbrella hanging over his head, a thunderstorm began. A perfect day to spoil a walk right before the first day of school!

    Things got so boring around here. He did not even go on a vacation this summer. His mother was way too busy to book a flight and pack the bags to go to Disney, his favorite amusement park.

    His mother wanted to go to Club Med instead. It was so boring. The last time he went to Club Med, he fell asleep in the pool and had to be dragged out by his dad. But for some strange reason, his mother loved the place because she did not have to do any work. She hated to run around Disney. High School Musicals annoyed her. The roller coaster irritated her. The food prices made her go mental! Just thinking about Disney made her dunk her head in the toilet.

Christopher chuckled as lightning flashed over the hill. He chuckled as he heard his mother roar at him to get back inside the house. He thought, *Mother is a very interesting person!*

His father was the total opposite. He loved Disney and hated Club Med. He said that Club Med was one of those places where people went in the 60's. The main attraction of Club Med was a sleep race and a eat race. In the bar, he even found a pair of ear plugs so people could sleep after becoming drunk.

Even though his Dad agreed with him, he was still wacky. In Disney, his Dad managed not to throw up at the Tower of Terror. In fact, he rode it two more times and was even able to eat his Angus Burger during the drop. He enjoyed the French Fries while going up. Then he sipped his soda while going down again. He was one risk taking guy. He was one crazy guy. Christopher's Mom almost fainted when she saw dad through the camera that was… you know, taping. He was way nutty and on film too.

Christopher thought about exactly how nutty his Dad was. Really he was not that nutty at all. Besides, he was just being reckless and having a good time.

His mother finally compromised and decided to go to their vacation house instead. That way she did not need to chase around people inside Disney and Christopher did not have to fall asleep in Club Med. The vacation house inside was fabulous. He remembered the house inside Ginn Reunion resort back in the summer between 3rd grade and 4th.

There was a water park inside the resort with miles of lazy river. The river was a huge circle of water that had a special current so you didn't have to swim. The current would just pull you around the circle. There was a part of the circle where there was a waterfall in which you would get splashed. In that part of the circle you would get drenched and chances are that you would fall off the tube.

Christopher would love to go to the vacation again this summer. However, just when they decided to go to the vacation house, her Mom's office had an emergency. The stock market was crushing. Companies were filing for bankruptcy. Her bank had many bad loans. She had to stay in the office to help

the bank that she worked for. Otherwise, her bank would have failed like Lehman Brothers!

Christopher understood the seriousness of her work and told her that he wanted to stay home this summer to work on his novel instead.

Christopher looked at the dark cloud and it reminded him of the train that zoomed through the track underground. He frowned because it reminded him of what was going to happen the next day. He was going to a new school.

But what's more, he was going on his own on the subway. He thought the subway was one crazy transportation system. He always thought that it was a miracle that it worked, but most of all that it was unbelievable that they even built it in the first place.

He closed his eyes and let the rains pour all over him.

Out of the blue, he suddenly remembered a pair of poems that he once wrote in second grade.

Rain

Twinkling down my arm a thrashing snail

Smoothly and gently rolls

down

my

skin,

And quickly another and another,

Soon the sky lights up with a million needles,

As I run back home,

My father says it is just rain.

Mud

It is a yard full of brown marsh like

Sticking mud,

All around

the

pigs,

Making a horrible glue for the farm,

"Spla, Splash SPLASH!"

Jumping in making a world of sticky brown marsh.

Chapter 2

The Dreams

Running into demons, devils, and angels... Racing his way through a path of lava... Seven people were guiding him.... Hundreds of people were helping him racing his way through doom.

It all started on his train ride, but then he woke up.

Christopher started to think of what just happened; the goblins, the angels, the seven headed unicorns, the fire breathing ogres. They all seemed real!

He saw himself riding the seven headed unicorns. He saw himself getting burned by the ogres. But at the end of the dream, he saw himself with a book, a plain old book with pages all shriveled up. A plain book! After all the unusual and crazy characters and animals, the end of it was just a book.

The dream was an amazing adventure, but it ended with a single plain book! It was something he could not describe.

The book was so shriveled up and crested. It looked like one of those old books from ancient treasure chests; books that you could only find in old buried treasures. It looked like something out of a fairytale. But yet, it looked powerful. It had some special text in it that he could not see yet with his bare eyes. Then he had a most unusual thought and he jolted off the fence.

Did the book exist? That was his thought.

Suddenly from that thought, the rain storm ceased. Christopher felt that he hit the jackpot. He used to think only the weirdest dream could have done that. Now he thought even looney ones could do things like that.

He laughed as he walked across the murky streets... back to his home. He rang the bell on his door. He was prepared to get yelled at by his mother. In fact, he was getting ready to get yelled at by his father as well.

The difference between his mother's yelling and his father's yelling was that his father's yelling was an encouraging yelling. It went like this. "Neat! Son, that's very gutsy of you. Great job." That was what Christopher called an encouraging yell.

His mother was a little different. Her yelling went like this. "What were you thinking going out in that storm…?" And that's exactly what she said as soon as he rang the door bell.

You could see she is a little bit less positive than his Dad. And that was usually how it went. His mother was screaming and yelling at him. And his father was encouraging him to do it again. His father loved taking risks and adventures, but his mother was all about safety. Christopher always thought: *how did these two get together and get married?!*

He was very happy that his girlfriend was actually sensible, unlike his mother. Her personality was more like his father, a risk taker, a positive supporter, and a lot of fun.

31

Another poem sneaked into Christopher's mind. It was one that he wrote in first grade to introduce his father to his class. Every one in the class laughed at it and it always cheered him up whenever he got into trouble with his dad. A smile finally came to Christopher's face when he remembered the poem again.

In the Bed with My Dad's Foot

I do not think my Dad's foot is pleasant,
But he keeps sticking up at me,

So I roll around,
And turn around,
But my father turned around,
With his foot pointing at me,

So I roll over again,
But my dad rolls over again,
With his foot sticking up at me,

And again, and again, and again
Until "Plop,"
I fall off the bed,
And "Plop,"
My dad falls on me.

Christopher giggled and knocked on the door again as he was waiting for his parents to answer.

He wondered who was going to answer first: his father or his mother. He hoped that his father would come to the door first. His encouragement was much better than his mother's criticism.

Chapter 3

'Twas the Night before the New School Year

$\mathcal{B}$ack to his bedroom, Christopher looked up at the ceiling.

He looked at baseball wallpaper on the other side of the room. Then he looked at his girlfriend's photo hanging on the wall. His eyes then rolled over to the guitar that he played. It hung against the wall opposite his girlfriend's photo.

On the right side of his guitar, he noticed a golden light shimmering. The small beam of golden light came from the window and softly glided to the wall. Seconds, later, he fell asleep.

Christopher never really understood what the golden light was, but again he saw it in his dream. He saw people teaming up together to fight many beasts. He also saw the golden light bouncing off a sword that a warrior held. The sword was a shining silver blade with a golden handle.

There stood a warrior who was also wearing an armor that he could not describe. It was a mix of gold and silver all around his body. But what he noticed most of all was that in his other hand he held the book.

With the sunlight bouncing off the sword, he noticed that the warrior had seven shadows. He was on the top of a mountain with seven suns beaming at him, all in different directions. Then he muttered something, "*Sava lamos*".

The sun's light stood still. Only the light that was already on the planet shone. The warrior's shadow vanished. Christopher noticed that his armor was full of cuts and scraps. His helmet looked rough and sturdy. He took off the helmet to look straight

37

into the seven suns. That was when Christopher knew that the warrior was himself.

The warrior muttered something and then said "*Rava lamos.*" Then the light returned, and his shadow appeared again. He slowly walked down the mountain, with a 2 headed eagle-like beast on his shoulder. Then he disappeared down the mountain side.

His dream focused on him again. This time he had a nasty cut cutting right down his left leg into his big toe. He snapped a leaf of a nearby plant and then said "Healio!!!" He grimaced in pain as he rubbed the plant onto the cut.

Saying just that one word took a lot of life out of him. Then, he went to sleep just like the real Christopher.

He actually saw a "12 hours later" sign in his dream! After that he saw himself again, but in his warrior form.

This time the long cut from his leg to his foot was gone. He got up and then stretching his newly healed leg, he started walking down the hill again.

* * * * *

Christopher suddenly jolted out of bed. He glanced at the clock near his bed. "10:05!" he said in surprise. He fell asleep at 10 o'clock.

"This is going to be a long night!" he thought. This is going to be the world's most boring night ever.

The night was long and hard. He wasn't able to sleep. If he did manage to sleep, the longest time he could sleep at would be 30 minutes. He knew something was going to happen in his new school, not just extra homework, he chuckled.

He knew that he was going to go with his friend tomorrow morning, so why should he be nervous?! If there were going to be any trouble in the new school, they would be with him.

Christopher finally was able to fall into a deep sleep at 1:00am in the morning. This time, his dream was different. He was getting sucked into a black hole with his girlfriend and two other friends. He also saw his enemy Jean Marie…

Chapter 4

The Morning

---

*H*oney! Honey! Christopher heard his mother call.

"Breakfast is ready, wake upppp…"

Christopher limped to the bathroom.

He slowly wet the towel and soaked it with soap. He squashed the towel until it was covered by suds and then washed it under running water. He flipped the towel onto his face, trying to wake himself up. He even tried to bump his head against the wall, but he could not get his dreams out of his head.

He felt like he was going to fall back into them. He wondered, what were all the dreams about? Why would they be there? There must be a reason.

He stumbled his way through the hallway to the kitchen as his mother was still hollering things in the kitchen. "Honey, if you don't get here now, I will personally go to your bed and spank your butt!"

Christopher ran over to the kitchen and started tapping on the kitchen table. He mother looked at him and asked, "What took you so long?" "It's a long… story… ." he said.

His mother gave him the breakfast.

42

"Hum, Yummy...smoked bacon and cheese omelet." Christopher was delighted.

He enjoyed his first-day-of-school omelet, which he always got in his 1st to 6th grade. After that, he even ate seven slices of lemon custard pie, his favorite. And they were not thin slices neither.

The first day tradition goes like this. At kindergarten, he had 1 slice of lemon custard pie. In first grade, he had 2 slices of lemon custard pie. In second grade, he had 3 slices and so on and so on. He really loved lemon custard pie. Those thick creamy slices with tangy lemon custard in the middle made his mouth water.

In fact, the custard was so juicy because his Mom added real lemon juice to it. The trick she used to make it taste great was to pour minute maid lemonade on it while it was warm from the oven and then serve it to him. The pie was hot, but the minute maid was cold. The contrast was sensational to the tongue and heaven to his tummy. He would cut off a corner of the pie crust and dip it into the minute maid

44

lemonade, which would become a cool syrup from the pie's heat.

He was on his fourth slice already. The only other times he was allowed to have that pie was once a month and on holidays. It was a family traditional treat. What's more? It was home made.

Christopher gave his Mommy a big (((hug))) and said, "Thank you for the delicious breakfast!" He also promised that he would pick up her groceries after school. He took his school bag and ran out into the street.

He would experience an adventure like no others.

Chapter 5

Friends Forever

---

*C*hristopher met his girlfriend, Julie Herring, while walking through the garden to the subway.

The two of them decided to stay together for the trip going to the school. They waited for the two friends, Max Fuzzi and Paul Beanstoc.

All of them walked silently through the garden until Paul started to talk. "Gee, I had a really really weird dream last night. I was in an archer suit complete with all the armors and stuff while a golden light bounced off the tip of my arrows."

"Freaky!" said Julie. "My dream was sort of like the same. The difference is that I was wearing spiked leather armour and had these attached metal claws on my hand. Amazing, a golden light bounced off my claws too," she muttered.

Finally, Christopher said something. "I had mostly the same dream that you two had, except that I had golden armour and I carried a sword. A golden light bounced off my sword too."

Suddenly Max piped up. "I think that all of us had mostly the same dream. Mine was a thin metal whip. As I swung my whip, a golden light reflected off the shinning metal."

"Did you have another dream after that dream?" Christopher asked.

"Yes," they all said. "We all got sucked into a black hole," they said at the same time.

"The thing is we were with Jean Marie. Do you think that this is actually going to come true?" Christopher nodded towards Max. Max nodded back.

"So you actually believe your dreams?" Julie and Paul asked.

"Well…yeah..," Christopher and Max said.

"Do you believe too?" Christopher questioned Julie.

"Only if you do," Julie said. "These things happen too many times in fairy tale." She declared.

"But what happens if it does come true?" Christopher asked. "Would we ever see our family again?"

Julie shouted in an almost berserk voice.

"Maybe and maybe not," Christopher said in a warrior's voice.

They walked to the subway chatting about the miracle dream. They thought that if it were true, it would mean disaster.

"Schools name is pretty neat," Max changed the subject. "Hunter College is a pretty name...a bit violent though… and it is not exactly a college but a middle school!"

Christopher chimed in. "I agree."

"Wonder whose idea it was to name a middle school Hunter COLLEGE?" Julie added as they made their way into the train.

Chapter 6

A Friend Who's a Girl

---

*J*ulie asked to be Christopher's girlfriend while in fifth grade.

When Christopher shook his head, she simply told him that she was a girl and a friend of his. By definition, Julie said, she was his girlfriend.

Christopher was a very reasonable person and had no choice but to accept Julie's logic. Since then, she was his girlfriend.

Julie was a gutsy girl. She laughed at things like when Christopher stuffed a grenade down an enemy's head in his d.s. war game. She got her guts from "handling" her two violent brothers. If she had a crush on someone, she would do one of two things. One was to go straight to the boy and said, "Hey cutie pie." Another way was to just look at all the bad parts of the boy.

Julie always tried the second technique first. The thing was that she found no bad parts about Christopher! She decided that he was going to be the first one to experience her "cutie pie" technique.

She had dark brown hair and wasn't exactly fat at all. (All the fat ran off while "handling" her brothers.) Her life was usually balanced. If one day she was super happy, she knew that sooner or later she was going to be in a tough spot. She was always prepared for things. On days that she felt sad though, she knew happiness would come back to visit again.

She was always able to dig herself out. That was what Christopher admired.

She put her head down on his shoulder on the subway. "The main categories were she and he, him and her, and his and hers." She thought approvingly as "he" laid his head down on "hers".

Slowly, out of the corner of her minds, he heard Paul whisper into her ear. "You are embarrassing us!" (Another thing about Julie is that when she was thinking in an interesting fashion she would, say her thoughts out loud.)

Julie blushed as she figured out what happened just then. Christopher did not blush or turn a deep red. He just chuckled and whispered into her ear. "You are an interesting girl."

Julie kept her head leaning on his shoulder. She turned even redder in the cheeks.

Christopher just smirked. Paul and Max laughed as Julie started to smirk also. They were one happy bunch.

Julie was the gutsy one. Paul was the shy one. He was unable to tell a fly that it was disgusting. Max, from Julie's point of view, glued the whole gang together.

But suddenly "FIRE IN THE SUBWAY, I REPEAT, FIRE IN THE SUBWAY!!! SHOOT THE ALARM!!!" screamed the train operator. "<JUMP

OUT OF THE TRAIN FOR YOUR SAFETY>" the
alarm boomed.

A sudden heat wave broke out into the train
and sparks started flying off the side advertisements.
Julie dug her fingernails into Christopher's hand

tightly. Max kicked open the window as Christopher recklessly jumped for his life out of the blazing vehicle.

Chapter 7

Fear and Courage

---

*H*elp!!! Max and Paul shouted.

There was a pole that pinned their legs down. "Wait here," Christopher said to Julie. "Take my hands." Christopher shouted to Max. Max flailed for a second and then grabbed Christopher's hand.

"Now hold Paul's hand." Christopher told Max. Max reached out for Paul's hand and then said, "I won't leave you, Buddy." Christopher shouted to the escaped passengers who were standing wide-eyed next to him.

"Don't just stand there, help me pull them out!"

Children helped tug Christopher. Julie and the adult tugged the children. A human rope started tugging Max and Paul. With all this force pulling Max and Paul back out, all their works paid off. Max and Paul suddenly tumbled out as the train disappeared in a ball of fire.

But below them, the track started to burn.

"Jump!!" Christopher screamed as he pointed to a burned out hole in the track.

"Chances are we'll be in a sewer. Just listen to the water drops," he said.

They all jumped in not knowing what to expect, not knowing what to think. In fact, they did not know what they were supposed to know. Suddenly they plummeted into water which was surprisingly very clean. If they thought they would never see   the sun jumping over the horizon, they were going to be wrong.

* * * * *

Julie suddenly opened her eyes, not knowing where she was. She slowly walked over to Christopher. "Hey, wake up, Chris!" (No answer)

"Hi, Cutie pie," said Julie in a nervous voice. Again, she heard no answer. Now she really got scared. She started to nuzzle his face. Then she started to nuzzle his ears.

Suddenly, Christopher started to open his eyes. "Wow!" he said while looking up. "Now, what's the deal about this place?"

"Christopher, you are alive!" Julie said in a cheerful voice. "But what do you mean about this place?"

"Look at the roof," Christopher said. Julie looked up. What she saw was something to take away her breath, something so amazing that made her almost faint.

The roof was made out of water. When she looked down again, she also saw the floor was made

out of water. When she looked around from every other angle, all she saw was water. That's when it hit her. They were in an air bubble.

Julie went carefully to Max and Paul to shake them awake. She was scared that they would die if she popped the bubble.

Max and Paul slowly got to their feet. In a minute or so, they knew just as much about the air bubble and Julie and Christopher did.

Luckily Julie knew how to survive in the water. Her cousin was a fisherman. He once invited her to a trip and showed her how to hunt fishes and catch crabs. She also learned how to catch shrimp.

She remembered the time she killed her first shark. It was smaller than she expected, but still weighted a good 120 pounds. It was a child hammer head shark!

She was as proud as the time she won the school spelling bee for the second time in that year. Two days later, when she learned to sail the boat correctly on her own, again she had that feeling of pride in herself.

Her achievements made her feel special. It made her feel unique. It made her feel superior. But she never used this against her friends. She called them personal accomplishments. They always paid off.

Chapter 8

Journey of Survival

$\mathcal{I}$f they wanted to live, they had to find a way out.

Christopher said to Max and Paul, "Stay here, we are going out of the bubble to look for some dry land. If not, this bubble will be our dry land,"

Julie said, "We will come back to get you."

Max and Paul did not know how to swim. They never learned to swim even though Christopher and Julie had tried repeatedly to encourage them to learn. Max was too shy to walk around the swimming pool exposing himself while wearing only swim trunks. Paul, on the other hand, was never given the opportunity to learn because his parents thought swimming was not necessarily a skill required to do well academically.

All that Paul's parents wanted was good grades in school. A grade of 90 was not good enough. It had to be a perfect score of 100. The pressure for Paul to do well in school escalated during 4th and 5th grades, when he needed the scores from the standardized tests to qualify for Hunter College's entry exam.

In all honesty, the pressure was not all from his parents. Paul knew that Christopher, Julie, and

Max would most likely pass the Hunter exam. He wanted to stay close with them in the same school. Already he had a broken family. If he could help it, he would not want to be separated from his friends.

His parents just wanted Paul to study, study and study more. There was no time for swimming lessons, no time for music lessons, and no time for baseball practices.

There was even less time for any other hobby after his parents divorced last year. Paul had to spend half his time living with his mother and the other half of his time living with his father.

When the Little League baseball coach asked Paul's Dad to bring him to the practice, his Dad replied: "Talk to his Mom." Then, when coach asked his Mom, his Mom said, "Ask his Dad."

In the end, Paul would miss all his baseball practices. When the team made the playoff, Paul felt he had not made any contribution to the team, but the funny thing was that his Mom, Dad, Stepfather, and Stepmother all showed up at the Championship game cheering him.

He felt so embarrassed when other parents asked, "Who is your son?"   All four of them answered, "Paul."

* * * *

Christopher and Julie went through the bottom of the bubble. They held their breath as the bubble reformed itself at the bottom where they got out.

67

They swam straight up. All they found was more and more water. So they started to swim down again. Then a golden gleam appeared at the very left edge of Julie's left eye.

With the remaining breath that Julie held, she gestured for Christopher to follow. As they got closer to the golden gleam, they noticed something. It was not just a something. It looked like a bunch of glass panels along a wall.

They looked through the glass panels and Julie thought she saw a manhole. She reached out at one of the glass panels and tugged at it. The manhole behind the glass panel suddenly cracked and plummeted down to the depth of the water.

An enormous wave of pressure cracked the glass panel at the same time. They felt the pressure suck them through the hole they had just made.

In just a few seconds, Christopher and Julie surfaced to the top of the water and took an enormous gulp of air.

Chapter 9

Doubts and Regrets

7hey saw daylight.

They thought they saw a police station across the street because there were a lot of police, firefighters, ambulances and emergency vehicles.

The firefighters looked tired. Their brown and rusting suits had black ashes all over them. Rescuers

lifted stretchers into the ambulances. Gasping as they ran across the street, Christopher and Julie yelled, "Help!"

A woman police officer turned and asked, "What's the matter, kids?"

"My friends are stuck below the manhole inside a sewer," Christopher said.

"Kids think of weird hiding places these days." The policewomen chuckled.

"Come on, seriously. There was a fire in the train. It burned through the track. In order for us not to get burned, we jumped into the sewer water, which was unusual because it was clean," Julie said.

"Ok...ok... let's go take a look. But if you are wrong, kids, you are going to be sorry. You are wasting a lot of time." The police officer disbelieved.

The police officer got some firefighters together. One by one, they jumped into the manhole with Christopher and Julie, swimming through shards of broken glass and slowly approached the bubble.

Something was wrong. Max and Paul were not there. Lying there in the bubble was a small pocket book. "What the..." The police officer screamed.

The officer skimmed through the pocket book inside the bubble. "Here, read this. I can not understand the symbols and all that stuff." The police officer waved to Christopher.

Paul and Christopher were always best friends. In fact, they even developed the codes for mutual communication. Within the last pages, he found a rock which had a code on it, too. However, there was no ink on the rock. Instead, Paul carved on the rock, probably because he did not have a pen with him. Or he worried that the water would rush into the bubble to wash off the ink.

"Now where could Paul and Max be?" Christopher said to Julie.

The code on the rock had only six symbols <I FOUND SOMETHING ON THE BOTTOM>.

"It said he found something on the bottom," Christopher muttered to the policewoman. "Follow me," Christopher said.

The police and the fire fighters followed him. Exiting the bubble, they dived down to the depth of the water. They were amazed at how clean and clear the water was. It just could not be a sewer! Everyone thought.

The policewoman started to believe these children.

As they sank, gravity took over and they started to fall to the bottom of the water, which they understood by now was man made. Amazingly, as they landed on the bottom, they found that they could breathe again. It was another vacuum bubble. In fact, they saw Paul and Max as well.

They were both blubbering and shaking. They were mumbling things like curse of the Gods. They were shouting things like "Huge wars…" They were rolling on the ground sputtering and they looked horror stricken.

If there were something that could scare even Max like that, it would have scared Christopher to death.

Max was the most courageous one among the four of them. He was the only one who did not

scream while watching the 3-D version of Godzilla. He was born with strength of courage in his blood. He was the only person in class who told the teacher that it might have helped her if she lost a few pounds.

He was the only one that patted the bee during science class. His family was just as reckless as he was. His parents took him to Africa safari for a hunting vacation when he was only a baby. In fact, Max was thinking about being the youngest to climb Mount Everest next year at the age of 12. Adventure was in his blood.

What could have made Max sputter rolling across the ground? He was bleeding.

The policewoman said, "Let's measure his heart rate… 170s per second… oh my God, better take him to the emergency room.

"Hey, what about the other kid, what's his name?" The woman officer asked.

"Paul." Julie answered. The officer measured Paul as well. "201 per second, we better get them to the hospital fast or they will die from heart attacks," the officer screamed.

"Hey, what's that?" Julie whispered to Christopher's ears, while pointing to the book he was still holding.

"It's the book that I saw in my dream," Christopher said as he opened it.

What he saw surprised him very much. He thought this was no time to explore as he put the book quickly into his pocket and rejoined the officer to rush his friends to the hospital.

One fireman dragged Max over his shoulder as he swam up towards the manhole. Another fireman grabbed Paul by the neck and floated him up towards the manhole. The police officer guided Christopher and Julie, thinking that they were children that needed to be protected.

They watched the bubble reformed behind them as they left and surrounded by water again. What were those bubbles? Were they new technologies discovered by scientists and were not yet known to the public? Did they find the new world? Did they enter a new dimension of the universe?

Plenty of questions accompanied their short trip back to the top of the manhole.

Chapter 10

Silence Unexplained

---

*A*s they surfaced through the manhole above ground, the policewoman told the other officers, "I have never seen anything like that."

"I can't believe we never knew about that manhole," She said. "We have to telephone your parents." The officer suddenly remembered. But

there was a problem. All they got was no connection through the land line and the cellular phone.

Julie was on the verge of tears.

"We will have to investigate your parents' houses," the officers said.

"What about Max and Paul?" Christopher asked.

"The hospital will call us. You have to find your parents first. Where do you live?"

"Briarwood," Christopher said, while holding Julie's hand trying to calm her.

The policewoman pointed to the police car and signaled the children to jump in. She turned on

the siren as she sailed through the city traffic and curious watching bystanders.

"Take these and put them on." The woman officer told them as he handed two pairs of ear plugs to Christopher and Julie. They listened and heard Paul's voice. The policewoman must have recorded Paul's staggering voice when they were underground.

"Good thinking, officer." Christopher complimented.

"Don't comment. Just listen," the officer commanded with authority.

Paul's tortured voice said, "Save the book... evil like no others..." Then the last word he said was "Noooooooooo!"

Right after that, the police officer got a call from the hospital.

"Both of them appear to be in a coma now, but they were awaked when they arrived at the hospital. They even asked the doctors what happened, but they hardly remember anything about the incidence in the train station. All they remembered was that they were on the way going to Hunter College High School. They were struggling to remember anything after they got on the train," the officer reported to Christopher and Julie.

"Are they OK?" Christopher asked.

"Yes, they are safe at the hospital. For some reason, they knew that something unusual had happened. The last thing they mentioned was that they found a book on the floor. When they touched it, they both blacked out," the officer told Christopher and Julie everything she heard from the hospital.

    They drove back to their familiar neighborhood. They saw the Key Food supermarket. Everything looked normal to their eyes, except that there were no people around.

There was no body at the cashier and no shoppers pushing carts around. As they walked through the deserted neighborhood, they approached their houses which were very close to each other, separated by a beautiful private garden with their favorite trees, shared by the community.

Max, Paul, Christopher and Julies were friends and their parents knew one another. When they were young, they used to place hide-and-seek in the beautiful garden. They still play hide-and-seek and giggled silly like babies.

In fact, Christopher's father let them build a tree house in his part of the garden. There were many childhood memories. Julie remember that they were all sacred of the toilet before they were potty trained.

That's how long they had been friends. They shared pain and happiness together. If one of them

was scared of something, the other three would also pretend to be scared of that, too.

Christopher remembered the time when Julie was scared of the boys' pee pee, so the boys pretended to be scared of pee pee too, so all of them just stopped doing it in front of her. They had to run back to their bathroom and locked the door first before pee peeing.

One day, they played outside all day and the boys did not pee at all. That night, Paul wet his bed during a nightmare.

Julie started to cry thinking of their childhood memories. She felt that were being torn apart as they grew older.

She had begged Christopher to come with her when her family spent the summer vacation in

Bermuda, but Christopher did not go. Neither did Chris go with Paul or Max. He just wanted to stay alone with his own family in New York.

The four of them used to be so close, but now they were drifting in different directions. They did not even tell each other their troubles any more, partly because they worried that they would cause the others sadness.

Coincidently on their own, each chose to keep silent of their every day worries and troubles, in an attempt to protect the others from sadness. In a way, they cared about each other too much to burden each other with unhappiness.

For once, Julie suddenly realized that their childhood happiness had long gone.

She wondered how it happened, but she knew the answers deep inside her. They had grown up and discovered that each of them needed their individual space of independence. They learned to respect each other's different opinions and different interests. During last year's spring, they had their first major argument.

It all started with the campaign for the Democratic Presidential nominee.

Although all four of them were Republican, they still took interest in the Democratic nominees' campaign. Christopher's favorite was Hillary Clinton, while the rest of them were voting for Barack Obama.

Christopher disliked Obama because he felt Obama was playing the race card during the campaign and he would divide the country instead of

uniting the country. Obama was more interested in the fame and glory, while Clinton was interested in serving the country. Besides, Clinton had the White House experience that Obama did not have.

The other three took the opposite stand. They disliked Clinton and blamed her for sending out the racially coded messages.

When Clinton was defeated, Christopher felt abandoned by his friends also. But they quickly mended the fence and moved on with their normal get together. They just avoid talking about the election all summer long.

Chapter 11

Dangers and Deadly

---

*T*hey arrived at Christopher's house first.

The police opened the door. "Mum...Dada?" Christopher called but heard no answer.

"Oh, no! Again?" Julie thought as she remembered her calling Christopher underneath the man hole with no response.

The officer searched through the dark rooms.

It was already early evening, but there was not the slightest hint of the familiar cooking odor from the kitchen. Even though it was his own house, Christopher was still scared of the dark. They searched every floor and went upstairs to search the roof. They even looked down the fireplace, but there was no sight of Christopher's parents.

Christopher started to whimper. He knew that his parents had taken a day off from work so they could greet him at home after his first day of school. That was the never broken family tradition. His mother should have been cooking in the kitchen, waiting for him to come home with the groceries.

There was one place where he dreaded searching the most. His father and mother did not let

Christopher and his friends play there. It was the basement.

That was the only place in the house where he was not allowed to go by himself because of all the family treasures kept there. The treasures were not valuable jewels or money, but little items that the family kept as memories.

They slowly walked down the stairs into the sea of darkness. The officer flipped on the flashlight. He still could not see that well. Why was it so dark in the basement? Suddenly the officers flicked the light on.

Julie laughed as she saw all his baby pictures.

She started to feel like a baby again when she saw the picture of Max, Paul, Julie, and Christopher. Memories flashed by. She was crying one day when she scraped her knee out in the garden. Luckily,

Christopher lent her a hand and helped her walk back to her house. At that time Max and Paul were already friends with Christopher.

After that, all four of them did everything together…almost everything.

They went to the movies together and even slept together sometimes in the garden. They counted the stars and made wishes to the moon in the tree house. They shared each other's dreams and comforted each other's nightmares. Very often they even had the same dream or nightmare after a long talk. It did not surprise them a bit because they were so much into each other's lives!

They remembered each other's birthday and celebrated them in their special way. They would get into a four way conference call on the phone right after midnight to sing the Happy Birthday song to the

birthday boy or girl. Then the birthday boy or girl would find a poem in their e-mail from each of the others.

On one of the walls, Julie saw a poem framed and hung in a beautiful hand carved frame. This was the poem that Julie gave to Christopher four years ago to celebrate Christopher's 8th birthday.

Christopher was born in April during the cherry blossom season. On Christopher's 8th birthday, his parents took him on a trip to Washington DC to catch the cherry blossom during the Spring break. They visited the Smithsonian Museums and the White House. They ate dinner at very fancy restaurants and took afternoon breaks in lovely tea houses and cafes. They watched the politicians rushing in and out of the Capital building and giggled while strolling through the Spy museum.

Then Christopher woke up one morning finding a blanket of snows on top of the flowers of the cherry trees outside the hotel window.

How often does one see cherry blossoms dusted in snow? It was one of the prettiest sights he had ever seen. He was overjoyed! He woke up his

parents immediately to go outside. His father took tons of pictures, of course. The three of them ran around the hotel garden like the happiest spring chicks.

It was a fun trip, but he missed his friends back home terribly. That night, just before his birthday, he arrived home in the middle of a rare April snow and couldn't wait to get on the phone with his friends at midnight to hear them singing Happy Birthday.

When he checked his e-mail anxiously, he found Julie's poem in his mailbox.

It was one of Christopher's favorite gifts of all. Julie did not know he had kept it and framed it along with his family treasures.

    She ran her fingers through the frame and glanced at Christopher with a smile.

Cherry Blossom

A cherry blossom hazily raining off a tree
to the ground,
staying with magic scents sticking
to them,

With a pinkish red hazy color,
flying around, falling on my head,
Softly not damaging me at all,
opening up, pealing off,

Running away from the other petals,
playing hide and seek with me,
Jumping off the tree,
dancing in the air with a very weak
jet pack,

letting gravity force the blossom to fall

down slowly,

Unwrapping an evil army of mites
to the ground,

Still I do not worry,
because I could always wash that away.

* * * * *

Christopher did not catch Julie's smile. In many ways, the boys did not treat Julie like a girl...until lately.

Julie laughed at the time the boys wanted to do everything the same way as she. They were almost identical after the hair project. Their parents

98

were awfully mad at them when they saw them come home with the same haircut. They still do a lot of things together, but they did not cry together or do those silly things anymore. And Julie grew her hair long nowadays.

* * * * *

Julie's childhood memories subsided as she glanced at another picture.

Drawn on the canvas was a picture of 9/11. Under it was the caption: *The Terror That Struck Again.*

"You don't think the same thing I am thinking right?" Julie said.

"I am afraid that I am." the police officer nodded. There were two words they now dreaded most: *Terrorist Attack*.

Chapter 12

Hope from the Past

𝓘t was crazy, nutty, twisted, and off the hook of Christopher's imagination.

He thought that nothing like this would happen in his lifetime. He also thought that if it did happen, it would not be he who was at the center of it. It would not be his loved ones running away from terrorist. It would not be his town suffering.

"Was there anything special over here?" Christopher asked, weeping because he would never see his mother or her special homemade pie ever again. He cried because he would never see his father juggle seven beach balls while riding a unicycle ever again.

He started crying uncontrollably for the first time in two years. He never felt so babyish in his life. He wanted to stop the tears, but he could not. He was not able to do so.

All the wetness in his eyes had been pumped out as tears. Every single bit of water in his body poured out of his eyes. He could not stop crying as all of his body's water poured from his eyes. His eyes burned but he did not care.

"I understand how you feel," said a wet eyed Julie. "Some things in life are harsh." She looked away from Christopher to hide her face.

"I never told you this, but my parents gave me up shortly after I was born. When I was old enough at the age of four, I heard that my real parents gave me up because they were divorced. I was heart broken. All the hope that they would take me back subsided.

"I cried without stopping for 4 days straight. On every single one of those days I locked the door and cried in bed. On every single one of those days I

refused to eat. I never went outside that door in those sad days. I had a bathroom in my bedroom if I had to…you know." She gave him a faint smile.

"I might have died of starvation if my adopted mother hadn't talked to me one day," Julie said.

"This is what my adopted mother revealed: 'When I was young, I lived the same life as you. Some things in life are not fair. They are what make a girl good and tough. They are things that make a girl stronger through life. Stop crying. I adopted you and I will love you forever as my daughter. No one will know that you are adopted if you don't want anyone to know. I am your mother from now on.'"

"'There is never anything that is hopeless.' My mother said. I am trying to tell you the same thing." Julie turned her face to look at Christopher in the eyes.

104

Christopher was shocked. He was taken back by the thought that Julie had actually kept a secret from him.

He would have never thought that to be possible. There were almost no secrets between Christopher, Julie, Max and Paul.

For the first time, he had doubts, but in a way, Julie's words gave him new strength. Julie trusted him with her most guarded secret and pain, for only one reason. She wanted to help him.

He could not let her down. Through tears, he thought that he could just cry all his life. Julie was right. He could save them! They had to save Julie's parents (adopted parents!), Max's parents and Paul's parents, too.

By now, Christopher and Julie were sure that all their parents were missing.

"Let's go." Christopher picked himself up.

"Good job, boy!" Julie said.

"Toughen up, kids.   Don't waste your energy crying, especially when you have important works ahead of you." The officer said.

"Yes. Madam," Christopher said.

"My name is Officer Thompson."

They slowly walked through the deserted streets. It was already completely dark outside.

Chapter 13

A Town Captured

*W*hat they saw they could not believe.

Not even the caterpillars sang their mournful song. The only sound they could hear was a racing police car riding toward the Briarwood police station. He wondered if even Paul would not be scared of this. Even the moon and stars were scared as they hid behind the clouds.

It was a silent night. The faint sounds of howling winds ceased as they rushed their way to their destinations.

The silence was dreadful. Even the police car's siren was quiet. There was no need for the siren as there were no people on the streets. The moon was their only companion.

Christopher always dreaded the silence. It absorbed all his awareness of what was happening.

At this moment it took all his awareness to the point that he forgot he was with Julie. Slowly, he slumped onto Julie's shoulder. Julie, too, was swallowed up by the darkness. Falling into Christopher's arms, Julie fell asleep.

Christopher did not move at all as he did not want to disturb Julie. She must be total exhausted!

He looked out of the car window at the moon in search for comfort. He found peace in its beauty. He always knew that music had an ability to calm him when he was stressed or scared. Now he realized that the moon had the same whimsical power as well when music is not there.

He closed his eyes and started a poem in his head.

The Music Moon

When the music moon hides in its den,
The earth is full of despair,
Though   if you sight this bright moon,

It is so equally fair,
So take it out of its lair,
And its piano music is so rare

Think of emotions,
Think of fine,
You would find it rather divine

It shows your feelings but hides your
thoughts,
It will teach you more than you were
ever taught,
It will show you more than you ever
sought... the Music Moon

Sink deep with its faithful sounds,
Enjoy all of its musical rounds,
Its breath spreads all over town... the
Music Moon.

* * * * *

Officer Thompson was talking on the phone while Christopher and Julie were asleep in the back seat. She was getting a report from the police headquarters on what had happened. She already drove by the local police station and found it empty.

The news she got from the police headquarters confirmed her fear. She was ordered by the commander to quickly get away from the town as soon as possible.

She felt responsible for these two kids now. She recognized Christopher and Julie as soon as he saw the poster on the wall inside Christopher's bedroom. It was a charity concert poster that she saw in a magazine two years ago.

She read that the benefit concert was organized by a group of fourth grade kids to raise money for children, so she bought a ticket to attend the concert with her little sister.

The concert poster was a picture of perhaps 20-30 children, all wearing white shirts and black pants or skirts. They were perhaps only 9 or 10 years old at the time. She could easily identify Christopher

and Julie standing in the middle next to a grand piano inside a concert hall, even though they looked a bit younger in that poster.

Christopher, in particular, was wearing a golden locket outside his white shirt. He was the only one in the group who wore an ornament, so it caught a gleam of reflection that shined on Julie standing right next to him.

She also recognized two other kids in that picture as Max and Paul. She should have recognized these children earlier, but all of them had grown much taller since she saw them in the concert.

The idea of organizing a charity concert came after Christopher did a school report on how the rising food costs had deprived the ability for humanitarian organizations to feed starving children in poor countries. He wanted to help.

Max, Paul, and Julie immediately rallied around him. They persuaded their music teacher to put together a concert program for the school chorus to perform. Many of their friends volunteered to perform. They sold hundreds of tickets to that concert. All ticket sales benefited the charities that help feed poor children.

Officer Thompson read that the concerts had raised a lot of attention as well as funds to help poor children. Some people did not even know that children were starving to death in poor countries, while we were throwing away food in this country. Many people, including him, did not know that it costs only 75 cents a day to feed a child in poor countries.

If even these kids could help so many others with their limited resources and power, Officer

Thompson was determined to make her influence tonight with whatever forces were under his control.

While in Christopher's room, Ashley Thompson had seen a picture of the concert poster on the desk. She had slipped it quietly into her pocket. She now reached one hand inside her pocket to feel the picture again.

* * * * *

"Wake up, kids," Officer Thompson called.

Christopher jumped up from his seat. "Are we there yet?"

"We have arrived." The officer pulled the car over to the main entrance of a hospital.

115

They came to the hospital because they needed to know what Max and Paul had found inside the bubble. Instinct told them that the train incident and the underground bubble held the clues leading to the sequence of strange events that happened today.

"I just spoke to people in the police headquarters… they said that the entire town of Briarwood had been captured or kidnapped.

"It happened so quick that no one knew what had happened until they lost complete communication with Briarwood's police station around 5pm in the early evening.

"They sent helicopters to fly over the town and discovered that the entire town was empty. We were searching in the basement of your house at that time so we did not hear the helicopters flying over.

"The police headquarters downtown had informed the White House. The President had ordered the army and air force to arrive as soon as possible. The FBI is on their way over to investigate as well." Officer Thompson spoke very fast, while running in the hospital hallway with Christopher and Julie struggling to catch up with her.

"So we have help on the way!" Julie and Christopher exclaimed, feeling a little relief.

"Don't count on it, kids. Let's be serious. They have never dealt with something like this in the past ----- none of us have!" The officer's words were not very assuring.

"I am sure it will be OK, now that the President and White House are in charge of the situation," Christopher said with more confidence.

Officer Thompson suddenly stopped in the middle of the hallway.

She did not even turn her head around. She waited till Christopher and Julie caught up behind

him.   Then she whispered very quietly so one could hardly hear.   "The President has been missing only minutes after he gave that order!"

All of a sudden, Julie thought her heart had stopped beating.   She held her breath.   Christopher turned to her and screamed at her.   "Julie, breathe, breathe, you have to breathe."

The officer finally turned around and came over to them.   "What's wrong?"

"She has asthma.   She is in shock and she can't breathe.   We need to get her medicine." Christopher ran over to the nurse not very far away and cried.   "My friend needs Albuterol please ----- she can't breathe."   Christopher was begging but he tried his best to remain calm.   He knew that she would die if he could not get her medicine immediately.

He now knew why the four of them had the same dream last night. It was a warning of dangers they would face ahead. He needed a cool head, or he would not be able to help Julie and the others.

She started to sweat. Her face turned all puffy and red. He wondered how she was feeling when she had attacks like this. The nurse was rushing down the corridor.

"Hang in there, Julie. The medicine will be here soon." Officer Thompson carefully laid her on the floor, while Christopher held her hand gently.

Within only a minute, the nurse came back with a doctor. She injected Julie's with an Epipen. The doctor checked her pulse and listened to hear heart. In very serious asthma attacks, Epipen is more helpful than Albuterol because Albuterol is an inhaler

which becomes ineffective if the patient can not breathe. Epipen, on the other hand, is an injection that can deliver medicine to the blood directly and quickly.

"I am OK, Chris. Don't worry." Julie told Christopher as soon as her breathing normalized.

"Why don't you rest here and wait for us? We will talk to Max and Paul upstairs and come back to get you." Christopher told Julie.

"Wait… we need to observe her for a while to make sure she is ok before she can leave. Are you her mother? You can't just leave her here," The doctor said.

"No, I am not her mother, Doc." Officer Thompson flashed her police badge. "We are investigating a very serious case. Please take care of

121

her. We will come back to get her as soon she we can."

"I'll come get you in a few minutes, Julie. Are you going to be fine here?" Christopher asked in concern.

"Go, Chris. I'll be fine…already feeling better. I'll wait for you here." Julie replied.

"See you later." Officer Thompson and Christopher screamed as they ran over to the elevator.

Chapter 14

Lost Brotherhood

---

*M*ax and Paul jumped up from their beds when they saw Christopher.

"Chris, where have you been? We worried about you and Julie."

"Julie is having a bit of an asthma attack," Christopher said in a small and nervous voice. "She will be okay, but what happened to you two?"

"It was a long story," Paul said. "We really did not know what happened. But for a few moments I felt like I relived my whole life again. It was happy. I could not think. I could not talk. I was not allowed to remember these things. I felt like a ghost. I was just watching a movie of me growing from baby to now. It was like a huge flashback… every single detail and every single dream…even all my feelings. All of them were stabbing at me. It took years for this flashback to end.

"Twelve happy years all in a flashback… I miss them. I even felt my body do things. I felt things like muscular aches, headaches, stomachaches; even love aches (crushes). I am really wondering if it really did happen. It felt so realistic, so life-like. I

really was living it again. I wish it would happen again. Of course there were those scary times when people yelled and those scary dreams. But everything was so happy…" Paul said dreamily. Water was building up in his eyes.

"I even got to see Mama and Papa together again before they divorced. Everything but one thing was revealed…." Paul began.

"That one thing: Who was that sibling?"

"You have a sibling?" Christopher asked. He never knew Paul had a sibling.

Paul nodded. " …You see, I once had a twin. But my parents gave it up. Who could it have been? I think I saw my twin, but I don't remember who it was. Besides that everything was so normal. The

thing is... Max did not have the same happy experience as I did."

Christopher turned his head, and to his surprise. He saw a shaking Max. Max cried. "It is a long story. It was something I can't describe. It almost feels like... destiny."

Chapter 15

Soul Bound

𝒫aul was brave and calm for a change but Max was crying for pretty much the first time in his life. What type of world was this?

Max was shaking while he tried to remember what happened. "First, I was trapped in a huge incinerator. Next, I was super small and running away from the hammers of a piano. Also, the piano

127

keyboard was endless. But then, the worst torture happened.

"Somebody ripped my soul. That was what it felt like. It felt like the time I got my foot trapped in the vacuum.......man.... It felt like the bottom half of my body got sucked by a vacuum. Plus, my top got sucked by another vacuum. My top was being pushed up while my feet were being pulled down.

"Soon my sides were being pushed towards left and right. It felt so horrible and then everything started burning and I got stuck by gazillion needles all over the place. Then I felt a gazillion volts of electricity were flowing through my body and I blacked out afterwards.

"The whole time it did not feel like a dream at all. It felt so real. I felt every single pulse going through my body. It felt like something turned a

switch and everything positive turned negative, while everything negative turned positive." Max began sobbing.

"Do you think you were hallucinating?" Christopher suggested.

"Perhaps, or I would have been dead." Max replied.

"Or maybe you are a zombie," Christopher joked.

"That's not funny. Not the right time to be joking," Max complained.

"Thing is everything positive became negative and everything negative became positive. I understand how you felt with those pain and burns,

but how were you able to feel the difference between positive and negative." Christopher questioned.

"That's exactly what I worry about, Chris. That is exactly what I fear."

"Do you think it means anything?" Paul asked Max and Christopher. "By the way, where are my parents? They should be with you when you came here." Paul started to realize something was wrong.

"And where are my parents?" Max asked as well.

Christopher hesitated and looked towards detective Thompson for help. The officer looked uncomfortably at Paul and Max.

He took a deep breath and said, "I want you to stay calm and be strong. This is going to be horrible news......."

* * * * *

"*W*hat?"

Paul and Max were shocked after they heard the whole story. "Are you saying our parents are dead?!" Paul whimpered after he heard the news.

"No, no, not dead, they disappeared." Christopher added in with a frown.

"Are you saying all the people in Briarwood disappeared?" Paul asked in horror.

"Yep..." Christopher said as he could not even find the energy to cry anymore. Christopher's Mom often said that he was a crying baby. Today he just realized that a person could no longer give a drop of tear when he felt so desperately exhausted and helpless.

Paul was feeling despaired. This was his worst nightmare ever! Max was feeling a similar way. He was listening quietly as he tried to process the information.

He also thought, "Why does this happen to me? After all of the happy times I had with my family and friends. I might never see my parents again!" But then Max asked the question. "Why isn't the president helping us solve this problem?"

Christopher hesitated and then slowly said, "'Cause he is gone as well."

132

Paul felt as though the entire world had collapsed on his shoulders. Suddenly he blacked out....

This does not feel right. Paul thought. His brain was able to think at ease but his body stared into the black hole. He felt too relaxed. He could move his body a little but not a lot. He felt weak, as if all his energy drained out of him. He had this experience before, but something made this so much different. It felt the same as always but yet, it felt different and unique.

Something very same could be very different if you think about it more. After a while he decided to give up on the idea. He decided that if he wanted to help his neighborhood he was going to need a plan.

Is it a sign of the end of the world? Something to mark our doom?

Then he remembered his own weakness, which was often pointed out by his parents and teachers. Paul tended to over react to things.

But this time he tried to stay calm. He had no choice because his parents were not there to fix his problems like they did every single time. So he had to rely on his own strength without his parents' presence.

This can not be the end of the world! So what could it be? A kidnapper? Oh, no! A kidnapper would not kidnap a whole neighborhood. So Paul thought about something bigger. That's when it hit him. Those three numbers…9-1-1.

What do you do when you are in deep danger? Where do you call when you are in deep danger? Why do they make it those three numbers? Paul's thought was racing randomly. The idea hit him with the speed of a jumbo jet going at max.

It is T-E-R-R-O-R-I-S-T-S. *Who else but the terrorists?!*

Chapter 16

Inner Strength

---

*H*e screamed as he woke up back in the hospital. "I think I know who did it," Paul said.

"Terrorists…." Christopher finished the sentence for him. "Julie and I thought the same!"

"You think that I am right? Christopher?" Paul was really not looking for confirmation.

Why couldn't Christopher say no? Paul always wanted to be right, but this time he would love to be wrong. Why didn't Christopher correct him?

"Yes." Christopher replied. "I was in the World Trade Center on the day of 9/11. And I thought this would never happen again." Christopher was dumbstruck by the thought once so vivid and alive again.

His memory flashed back to seven years ago when he was only five years old.

* * * * *

Christopher was visiting his Mom's office at work in the World Trade Center.

137

Happily they jogged to the elevator and Christopher jumped up and down as the elevator lurched up to the thirty-six floor. They got out of the elevator and his mother flashed her company ID to the security guard. The nice security guard smiled and let them through.

"Now who is this little critter?" the security person said jokingly to Christopher.

"I am my Mom's little baby." Christopher replied in triumph.

"Uh-Huh," His mother said. She sounded both bright and proud.

His mother was a trader at a bank. She was also a banker. She had two jobs.

Basically, as a banker, she lent money to companies like Apple, Starbucks and Google. The companies would take the money to make the products for sale. They would return the money with interests to the banker who lent them the money. If they could not sell the products they made, the company would not be able to return the money and they would have to file for bankruptcy. In that case, the banker like Christopher's mom, would lose her job.

She was also a trader so she would trade the stocks on different companies. Basically, the companies would share their profits with the stockholders. So his Mom's job was to pick the stocks of companies that she believed would sell a lot of products to make profits. If she picked the wrong stocks on companies that did not make profits, she would lose her investment.

Obviously the more research the banker and trader does, the better the chance that she would pick the right stock to invest. That makes the difference between a good trader and a bad trader.

Christopher's Mom was a good trader and banker.

Normally, a good banker and trader would travel around to visit the companies that they lend to or invest in so he would know if he made the right decision. For example, Christopher's Dad, who was also a trader, had to go visit the Apple and Starbucks stores when he invested in Apple and Starbucks stocks.

For some reasons, his Mom was able to do well without visiting the companies.

Christopher's Mom did not like to travel because she wanted to spend time at home taking care of him. She just begged her co-workers to travel to visit the companies for her. She was particularly grateful for her co-workers to help her with her jobs so she could spend more time raising her baby.

Her co-workers were particularly fond of the cute little Christopher that they did not mind traveling for his Mom. Over the years, they became very good friends.

When one was sick, the others would pick up the work load. When his Mom needed to take a day off to attend Christopher's school play, her friends covered for her.

Likewise, when her friends broke up with their boyfriends, his Mom would take them out to lunches and dinners to heal their broken hearts.

141

Not only were they colleagues, they were also the closest friends.

On the morning of 9/11, Christopher went to her mother's office because it was his Mom's day off and she wanted to stop by the office to check on work before taking Christopher to the library.

It was not Christopher's first time to his mother's office.

When he was only a baby, his Mom would take him into the office when she worked over the weekends. The office was empty on Saturdays and Sundays. She would put his favorite blue baby blanket on the floor with a few toys. Christopher would play on the floor by himself while his mother worked. When he got tired, he would fall asleep on the floor.

By the time Christopher turned three years old, his Mom would let him play on a computer set up with games. His mother would work on her computer while Christopher worked on his.

One time, Christopher asked his Mom what she was doing on the computer. His Mom replied, "Why? I was working hard to make money of course!"

Christopher looked at his Mom with disbelief and said, "Mom, can I work on your computer next time?

"Why? What's wrong with your computer?"

"…WELL … mine did not make any money!" Christopher replied with disappointment.

His Mom laughed so hard and he did not understand why at the time.

They had a lot of happy time in his Mom's office in the World Trade Center.

This morning on 9/11, they were going to visit her mother's office briefly. It was so early in the morning that only a few people arrived at work.

"Hello, Chris. I have not seen you for only two months and have grown so handsome. Look at those beautiful eyes. Would you be my boyfriend when you grow up?" A pretty girl teased him. Joyce was her mother's colleague.

She was a young stock analyst who had been working with his Mom for four years. She adored Chris and played with him whenever he came to visit the office.

"Ok, Joyce. You will be first in line to be my girlfriend when I grow up." They laughed and giggled.

Joyce then took out a piece of jewelry and casually handed it to Chris. It was a golden metal necklace with an ornament engraved with an ancient symbol.

"I found this necklace in the staircase this morning and no one in the office recognized it. It is a locket. Why don't you keep this as a good luck charm?"

"Oh! Thank you, Joyce. You are my best girlfriend. I will wear it whenever I need some luck." Chris thanked Joyce cheerfully.

They spent only 15 minutes in her Mom's office and decided to go downstairs for breakfast.

There were many restaurants on the ground floor of the World Trade Center. There also were a lot of shops.

Le' Croissant was his Mom's favorite, favorite restaurant. Flaky delicious croissants those were creamy and soft on the inside. Stuffed with chocolate so fluffy and rich! The sweet vanilla crust and the bitter chocolate made an amazing bitter sweet taste that was enough to make his Mom cry. There were also the strawberry croissants, these had sweet natural strawberries crushed and lightly fluffed up into the croissant.

* * * * *

Christopher was starting to get happy tears as he imagined how amazingly good they were.

"So, we decided to have 2 croissants for breakfast…" Christopher recalled while Paul and Max were listening. "It was the croissants that saved our lives in the World Trade Center." Christopher paused.

"When we got downstairs, the line at Le' Croissant was already very long because thousands of people were getting into World Trade Center to begin the work day. We waited in line to get our croissants. My Mom also got a coffee for herself and a juice for me.

"As soon as we sat down to take the first bite, we heard some people screaming for everyone to evacuate.

"We did not know what had happened at that moment, but my Mom, who had experienced a fire that burned down her house when she was only three, grabbed my hand (and the croissants as well☺) and ran outside. We thought it was a fire.

"As soon as we got outside, my Mom found a phone booth and tried calling her colleagues upstairs to tell them to get out. No one picked up the phone.

"Just when my Mom contemplated to go back into her office again to tell them, the building started to collapse across the street." Christopher wiped a

tear.

"Chris, you never told us about this!" Paul and Max exclaimed. They thought they knew everything about one another. The idea of Christopher keeping this a secret from them meant only one thing.

It must be something that Christopher never wanted to remember. It must be a horrible experience that he tried to forget. Poor Chris!

"Don't worry about me. I am all right." Christopher took a deep breath and looked firmly into the eyes of Paul.

A very gentle smile appeared on Max's face. He reached out his hands to Christopher and Paul. The three of them held their hands tightly in silence.

"Time softens most pains even if the memories are not erased," Christopher said. "Those who died did not get healed, but those who survived had moved on with their lives."

"It does not mean the memories went away, but the pain had become more tolerable with the passage of every day going by. It took a long time for Mom to grieve for her friends, but she ultimately found the strength to recover and continued living happily every day.

"If anything were to happen to our parents tonight, I hope we will be able to find the strength to live on...." Christopher suddenly stopped himself from continuing.

"This is why you told us the story tonight?" Paul asked.

"My Mom told me that life is never constant. The only constancy is the unpredictable changes we experience every day. Because the phenomena of changes (joy, pain, lose, gain, etc.) is a form of life, we have to experience all of them if we want to live life to its fullest.

"But it does not mean we are giving up on saving our parents and friends tonight, even if we have to prepare for the worst to come tomorrow." Christopher explained.

"Understood."   Paul and Max nodded to assure Christopher.

Officer Ashley Thompson stood at the corner of the window and thought to herself. "Why didn't someone tell me this before? Would my life be any different if my Mom told me this when I was a girl? Would I have made the same choices?"

Out of the corners of her eyes, Officer Thompson cast her doubts. She soon would have to tell them. The thing is that she was forced to do it…

After spending only a few hours with these kids, she no longer found the strength to carry on her plan. What had happened to her? Did she find the kids? Or did she get captivated by them?

She shook her head to wake herself from these kids' enchanting spell. Sadly she remembered her

family. They needed her! Even though it was her family, she had doubts, if she wanted to do her job to get her family back?

Chapter 17

A Book of Hints

---

*C*hristopher walked out of the hospital inhaling the sweet morning air.

The sun was just peeking out at dawn. He saw the birds happily flying out of the window.

He did not sleep all night and his head was pounding. He was physically hungry and exhausted.

By instinct he reached inside his pocket to search for something to eat, perhaps a candy or even a piece of gum that he usually kept inside his shirt pocket. Then he laughed at himself. How could there be anything edible after swimming in the sewer yesterday?

A heavy lump weighed his shirt down. He gulped as he suddenly remembered the book that he found inside the bubble within the sewer.

Slowly his sweaty hand reached down into his pocket…. and slowly came back up. Looking at the cover he hesitantly turned to the first page. Swiftly, a letter drifted out of the book.

Christopher snagged it right before it touched the floor. Written on the letter Christopher saw:

"There's a hag and a fool,

An Enemy for me...two for you,

Do you think it's possible?

Do I faze you?

Do I scare you enough to get you ...

Blasting to the moon?

If so, I am following your tail,

Be warned, I am stalking you."

Christopher was puzzled. He looked at Julie and handed the letter to her.

Officer Thompson was talking on his cellular phone next to the police car parked about 20 feet away. They could not hear his conversation but he looked very upset.

"What's that?" Paul and Max asked.

They were both released from the hospital after the doctors checked them out. Julie was released as well, after a few hours of rest. Officer Thompson explained to the doctors that the police needed these kids to help search for the missing people. By now, the crisis was all over the news. The doctors reluctantly released them knowing the police needed these kids' help.

Meanwhile, there was a huge jumble of thoughts crashing in and out of Christopher's head. Max wondered why all these things happened to them.

"Why would the terrorists capture the whole neighborhood? Where could they have hidden them? Are they even still alive? What about the President? He is gone too?" Max asked the rest of them, but it sounded more like he was thinking out loud.

"There's a hag and a fool…" Christopher kept repeating those words. "What could it mean?" Christopher would always figure things out, but this time he had not even a clue.

Julie guessed, "Chris, it sounds like someone is after us. I hope the terrorists are not aiming for us."

"Why is it always us?" Christopher, Julie, Paul and Max said simultaneously.

"Well, it's not just the four of us in trouble. The whole neighborhood is in severe trouble. At least we have a fifth person joining our little clan," Julie said.

"A fifth person? Wait the minute. There is a hag and there is a fool. If we are the fool, then where is the hag?" Max suddenly chirmed in.

"The hag has been FOLLOWING us very ----- - closely," Christopher said in a very low but calm voice. "I think I know who she is and you know who it is too."

"Well, I have a good suspicion too," Julie said. "But it is only suspicion. The thing is it does

not make sense. She would have been done with us already if she is the hag."

"I agreed with you. I think that when you guys are hungry and tired, you start to imagine crazy stuff." Paul contradicted Christopher's theory.

Christopher took a glance at Officer Ashley Thompson far away and quickly turned the pages of the book. The rest of the pages were hand written notes in a different language than English. Only the poem that fell out of the book was written in English.

"Can any one of you read this language and understand what it means?" Christopher was frustrated.

Julie took over the book and shook her head. "It is certainly not English, Italian, French, Spanish or

Latin." Among the four of them, they each knew a foreign language.

Then Max jumped and grabbed the book from Julie's hand.

"Look at the drawing on this page. The symbol looks very familiar…" Max said.

Paul looked over.

"You are right, Max. Where have I seen it before?" Paul also recognized the symbol.

"It's the symbol engraved on your locket, Chris." Julie took a look and screamed.

"You mean the necklace that Joyce found in the staircase of World Trade Center on the morning of 9/11?" Christopher looked over the page.

161

"She gave it to me as a lucky charm. It was the last gift she gave me and I still wear it from time to time whenever I feel I need some luck. I feel as though she is an angel looking after me when I wear it." Christopher could not believe it.

"Where is your locket now?" Max asked Chris. Chris immediately grabbed the shirt on his chest, but there was no necklace.

"I don't know. I wore it to the first day of school yesterday and now it is missing." Chris sounded more frustrated.

"You probably lost it when you were swimming underneath the sewer." Paul suggested. "I faintly remember that you had it on when we were still inside the bubble. I saw a golden light

shimmering. The small beam of golden light was probably reflection from your locket"

Christopher suddenly remembered his dream and murmured, "I now understand what the golden light was in my dream! The warrior in the dream was actually myself."

"Chris, we have to retrieve the necklace. I am afraid there may be a connection between the necklace and everything that is happening..." Julie said.

Chapter 18

The Angel Watching

---

*O*fficer Thompson finished her phone call and was walking toward them. Julie quickly slipped the book inside Christopher's pocket.

"Officer Thompson, can we go back to the sewer under the subway please? ...Umm..." Christopher was struggling to find an excuse.

"No, kids. You are going nowhere. The police headquarters needs to question you," Thompson said.

"Chris…" Julie whispered. "The police headquarters is not that far from the sewer. I can pretend to go to bathroom once we get there, but instead I can go search in the sewer."

"No…Julie. That's way too dangerous. By the way, it's my locket so I should go get it." Christopher insisted.

"But you are the center of their attention. It looks like they want to question you more than me. After all, Thompson searched your house first, not mine. I've got a hunch that she was looking for something she needed…perhaps the locket…" Julie murmured.

"Julie, are you saying she is the hag?" Christopher whispered in wonder.

"The situation just got crazier by the minute. And that's only thing that I am saying," She said.

"What? This is not the right time to make jokes, Julie. You are accusing a police officer of being a terrorist."

"Yah, but what happens if she is really a terrorist?" Julie said.

"I would never believe our police officer is a terrorist." Christopher still denied the theory, even though the same thought flashed through his mind earlier.

The car was approaching the police H.Q. They stepped out of the car. Julie announced that she

had to go to the bathroom. Christopher immediately said he had to go, too.

"What is this? How old are you kids?" Thompson teased them. "You still have to raise your hand and go to the bathroom together? You two act more like kindergarteners."

"Just make it snappy." She ordered them in a stern voice. This was the first time that Christopher detected a little annoyance in Ashley Thompson's voice.

Christopher and Julie just ran down the hallway toward the bathroom on the right. Instead they made a left turn and exited through the large window.

They ran for a minute across the street and found the water hole where they escaped yesterday

morning. There were police tapes sealing the hole, but no one was guarding the scene. They quickly jumped into the water and swam their way back to the bubble that they had found. Sure enough, there was a shiny piece of metal on the bottom of the bubble. Julie swam a long way ahead of Christopher and got inside the air bubble first.

Christopher was a lousy swimmer until Julie taught him last summer in the community pool. He almost drowned in the beach one summer. Julie was determined to teach him the right technique.

At the beginning, Christopher hardly ever wanted to take a lesson from a girl. He was plenty embarrassed to have a girlfriend, let alone having to have a girlfriend coach him in swimming. How much worse could it be than that? He also did not want her to see him in his swimming trunks.

168

Julie had to drag him to the pool every Sunday, while he kept on screaming, "I would never get coached by a girl. Hear my words. I said NEVER…"

"Pretend I am a boy then," Julie said.

"I don't want you to wear only swim trunks like a boy. Privacy is important in my family." Christopher laughed.

The next week, Julie showed up at Christopher's house with a brand new bikini. Christopher rolled his eyes and they walked over to the pool.

"You can never be a boy. You care about fashion too much. We boys DO NOT."

"Well, I have something to say to you then. You can never be a girl. You boys care about cooties too much. We girls DO NOT."

They laughed silly but Julie finally convinced Christopher. They had so much fun swimming in the pool every Sunday. Julie was a good teacher and Christopher was a good student. They always went out to have ice cream after the swimming classes. By the end of the summer, Christopher could swim very well, if not as good as Julie.

Julie was a good teacher, but even she could not teach her student to be as good as she. Christopher was great at playing piano, so he tried to teach Julie in exchange, but for some reason Julie's fingers did not exactly find piano to be a good companion even though Julie, herself, loved the music made from the piano. Perhaps she just loved the music that Christopher made from the piano.

Soon enough, the piano lessons stopped and Julie decided to pick up singing instead. She turned out to be a pretty good singer and sang a beautiful solo at the benefit concert. Everybody has different talents.

* * * * *

Julie was the first one to get to the necklace.

She picked it up and examined it closely. She recognized the symbol. The symbol was the same one as the diagram drawn in the book. She admired a ruby that sat in the middle of the symbol, but then she remembered there was no ruby drawn in the diagram. She pressed the ruby hard but nothing happened.

"Christopher, can I pull the ruby out?" Julie asked Christopher for permission as soon as he got inside the bubble.

Christopher caught his first breath inside the air bubble before answering her. "Yes, Julie."

Julie carefully pulled the ruby out by using her nails. The pendant immediately sprang open.

Their hearts raced and pounded when they saw what was engraved inside the locket.

* * * * *

September Repeats
Doomsday
Let Civil Kill Themselve

Julie and Christopher looked at each other and knew instantly that this locker would hold the secret to save them and the others. Finally, they found a glimpse of hope. *Joyce was the angel watching over him!* Christopher thought.

Chapter 19

The Hag Peeks Her Head

---

*A*shley Thompson was impatient. "Those kids are taking a long time to go to the bathroom," she said.

"Christopher enjoys reading while sitting on the potty," Paul said. "So does Julie." Max added.

"Uh-huh…" Thompson said half-not-believing them. "I am going to check them out."

Just when Thompson turned her head toward the bathroom, Christopher and Julie popped up in the hallway.

Suddenly Thompson put on a new stern look from the corner of her eyes. She gritted her teeth and asked the kids, "What took you so long?" Her eyes were locked on the pendant worn on Christopher's neck.

Christopher intentionally put his locket inside his shirt right in front of Thompson's eyes. Thompson asked Christopher, "Where did you find that pendant?"

"Why do you ask? I had it in my pocket and I just put it on for good luck." Christopher replied.

"Oh... now follow me to the questioning room." She knew what she had to do with Christopher. Sadly, Thompson knew that it was going to be more than questioning that she had to do. She had to complete her mission tonight if she wanted to ever see her family again!

"Officer Thompson..." Christopher said as he took out the book he found inside the bubble.

"Chris..." Julie tried to stop him. Christopher looked at her with a twinkling eye and suddenly Julie understood.

"Remember this pocket book? It belongs to you," Christopher said.

Thompson took a look and immediately said, "That's not my book. We found it together inside the bubble."

"Are you sure you did not drop it accidentally or perhaps intentionally?" Christopher asked as he looked at Thompson's police badge hanging on her shirt. "Is your name Ashley Rose Thompson?"

Officer Thompson was silent but looked as if she was paralyzed in fear. Julie ran her hand over the book cover, which had three letters written on it.

"Aren't **A.R.T** your initials? What a coincidence?" Julie scorned.

Suddenly, Ashley Thompson took a quick look around and kicked the kids into a dark room.

"What's the matter with you?" Christopher blurted out in pain.

"I am sorry kids, but you have to give me your locket. I promise that I will not hurt you…I just need your locket." Thompson hollered, but somehow it sounded like begging more than threatening.

Max and Paul were speechless. "Are you the hag?" Paul asked. "And are we the fool?" Max took the remaining words out of Paul.

Thompson gave up as she slouched into the chair next to Christopher. "I never wanted to harm you from the start. You are all very good kids with kind hearts.

I would never hurt you if I had a choice….but my family depend on me!" She buried her head into her hands.

"Tell us your problem…we may be able to help you," Paul said. "Trust us and trust yourself if you don't really want us hurt." Max encouraged him.

"Look, it is not just our lives and your family's lives. It is the lives of thousands of innocent people." Julie pressed him firmly. "And don't forget the life of our President. He is the leader of this country. Without him, our whole nation is at stake."

Thompson lowered her head pensively. She pondered whether she should tell the truth.

"I had no choice. One day, I received an anonymous letter and a book." Thompson began.

"Is this the letter?" Christopher took out the poem from his pocket and gave it to Thompson.

"Yes. This is the letter. I did not know what it really meant. Soon, I received a phone call. The caller did not identify himself. He claimed that he had taken my family hostage right under my watch. They were the ones who trashed my life.

"I was told to look for a locket that he lost many years ago in the World Trade Center twin tower. The book had a picture of the symbol to identify the locket that I was supposed to look for.

"I had no clue what to do and where to look at the beginning.   My family has been missing for almost a year now. I am the hag… and also the fool." Thompson sounded very sad and desperate.

"And you did not tell anyone or ask for help?" Christopher shook his head unbelievably.

"They would kill them if I said anything. They promised to release my family if I found the locket," Ashley Thompson said.   Her eyes looked a bit watery.

She slowly turned away from the kids and then continued, "I was really hopeless until I saw you running to me for help after the subway explosion. When I saw you and Julie, it rang the bell in my head. I saw your concert a year ago and I suddenly remembered seeing the pendant on your neck in a concert poster.

"I was still unsure that you were the kid in the concert wearing the locket, so I tested you.

"I dropped the pocket notebook deliberately inside the bubble. As you flipped through the pages, I was watching your face to see if you had recognized the symbol drawn in the notebook. But you did not recognize it.

"So I thought you were not the boy in the concert." Thompson confessed. "After all, you had grown a lot over the last year."

Christopher felt sorry for Thompson. He offered her an explanation. "The truth is I did not flip through every page. I missed the page with the drawing so I did not see the symbol," Christopher said.

Thompson nodded her head and said, "I thought I had misidentified you. Then when I saw the concert poster in your house, I was very certain you were the boy wearing the locket in the concert."

Christopher was disappointed at Thompson and confronted her. "You did not kill us only because you needed me to find the locket."

Thompson felt shame. She cried, "No, no. I would have never harmed you. I wanted to find the locket so that they would release my family. But I also wanted to help you find your parents and all those missing people."

Something did not feel right. Her feelings twirled into a big headache in her head. "But I could not let you stop this plan. My family would die and it would be all your faults."

"What plan? So you know about the terrorists' plan for capturing the entire town?" Max confronted Thompson.

Thompson shook her head and replied, "Not really, at the beginning I believed that all they wanted was this pendant... and they would release all the innocent people, including my family, if I found the pendant for them. But now I am not that sure anymore."

"Chris, you must give them the pendant to save these people, no matter how valuable the pendant is." Max was pleading with Christopher. He felt sorry for Thompson, too.

Christopher shook his head. "No, Max. I don't think that would save the people."

"What do you mean? Chris?" Max asked.

"You don't think they want the pendant?" Paul and Max had the same question.

Julie suddenly interrupted while looking at Christopher. "No, I think they do want the pendant for sure, but they would not release the people. They want the pendant for a different reason…"

Chapter 20

The Symbol

"*J*ulie is right," Christopher said with a sigh.

"Why would they want the pendant so much?" Paul could not help but join in. "There must be a reason, right?"

Christopher held the locket and stared at it hard and cold for the first time. He never really

looked closely at the pendant before today. Because the locket was a gift from Joyce, his mother's friend and co-worker who was killed in World Trade Center, he really did not care how it looked like. All that the pendant meant to him was the memory of Joyce.

"What is it? Chris?" Julie asked.

"The symbol... I think I saw it before." Christopher suddenly gasped.

"Where?" they all whispered, gritting their teeth.

"The Olympic Game during the opening ceremony…" Christopher took a deep breath.

The 2008 summer Olympic Games were hosted by China for the first time in history.

China is a very interesting country. It has 5,000 years of history and culture. It has tremendous natural resources in oil, metals, woods and land. It also has one-fifth of the World's population.

Nevertheless, the country was a mystery to the Western world because of its political situation in the last hundred years.

China had always been ruled by kings and emperors until early 1900s when the Communist

government took control over the country. The Communist government at that time believed in sharing equal wealth among the rich and the poor. When people objected, they would be put into jail or killed.

Because of that, the country became very poor. Many Chinese people even escaped from the country.

When other countries objected to China's policy, the Chinese government decided to close the country to the Western world. They did not allow people from other countries to visit China anymore. That made China so mysterious to the rest of the World.

The Chinese culture is very rich and deep, but the rest of the world did not get the opportunity to understand it.

That situation changed in the late 1900s when the old government died. The country opened its doors to the Western world and shared its culture once again. The Communist government also threw away its equal wealth policy and adopted the Capitalism policy which rewards people who work hard with more wealth. Basically, the harder you work, the more you earn.

Chinese people are recognized as some of the hardest workers in the world because of its culture. Under the new policy, the new China was blooming and becoming wealthy again very quickly. The rest of the world was dazzled and fascinated by its culture and history.

They were hungry for the knowledge of the old and new China. They could not believe how fast China had changed in the last few decades. In only

two decades since it opened its door, China had emerged from a very poor third world country to become a leader of World power, standing shoulder to shoulder with the United States.

The Olympic ceremony demonstrated how deep, beautiful and rich the Chinese culture is. It also showed the world, for the first time, how amazingly powerful and wealthy the country has become. Those who remembered China as a poor country only a few decades ago could not be more amazed.

Athletes who competed in the Olympic Games took inspiration from the magnificent Great Wall of China.

Any one who has seen the Great Wall would be overwhelmed by its sheer mass of inhuman power. If the Great Wall could be accomplished thousands of years ago with human hands, what could not be attainable? So the athletes thought!

The country's glory in culture and beauty was celebrated by the entire world during the Olympic Games. The new China's grandeur is not only found in its newly obtained wealth and glory. It stunned the world with its sophisticated resources, people and talents.

Christopher remembered how amazing the opening ceremony was. He was glued to the TV for four hours with the rest of the world.

The world was watching with such long awaited hunger, devouring every moment of the jaw dropping beauty in details.

It was generally regarded as the best Olympic Games opening ceremony in history. China should be very proud for gaining that title.

Not known to many people including Christopher, a lot of modern day technologies were actually invented by ancient China a few thousands years ago. The opening ceremony tried to showcase some of China's many inventions like firework, silk making, martial arts and book printing.

Printing was such an important invention because it promoted communication, advanced teaching and accelerated civilization for the whole world.

The Chinese devoted a very important segment of the opening ceremony to celebrate its achievement of inventing the printing machine.

In one segment of the opening ceremony, there was a scene of thousands of people (dancers and soldiers) hiding inside thousands of blocks to simulate the movement of a printing machine.

The movements were so amazingly even and realistic that the whole world thought the Chinese characters and symbols displayed by the blocks were operated by computer and machine. No one had expected that the few thousand blocks were operated in synchronization by humans hiding inside the boxes.

One can not imagine the surprises when thousands of soldiers and dancers popping out from the boxes at the end to show the world what an "inhuman" task they had accomplished. The Chinese had the entire world fooled and amazed!

Christopher's father had recorded the opening ceremony and the two of them had watched it over and over again many times.

"The symbol is the Chinese character standing for HARMONY," Christopher said. "I saw it in one of the segments of the 2008 Summer Olympic Games opening ceremony."

"My God! Now that you mention it, I seem to remember as well. It was the segment with dancers simulating a giant printing machine," Ashley Thompson screamed out at the same time.

"Why would a Chinese symbol have anything to do with terrorists?" Max asked.

"And the symbol 'HARMONY' seems to contradict the current dangerous situation." Paul added. "What do the Chinese have to do with all this?"

"No, no. The Chinese always worried about the West attacking its country. That was why they closed the country from the West a few decades ago." Officer Thompson suddenly said. "Although they had opened the country to the West again in recent years, they are always skeptical that other countries would rob their resources and wealth."

Max was confused with Thompson's explanation. "What is your point? Are you saying that the Chinese are paranoid?" Max was obviously impatient with Thompson.

Paul was annoyed as well. He did not appreciate Thompson's explanation and said, "This is not a surprise. China had been taken advantage of many times in history."

Thompson knew the children were confused by her, so she explained further, "The Chinese government had very well trained spies, sort of like our CIA in the United States.   They spy on activities of other countries to make sure China was not a target for attack." Thompson explained. "Besides, potential terrorist attack on China during the 2008 Summer Olympic was a major concern of the Chinese government."

"Let me guess.   You think this locket belonged to a Chinese spy who had information on the terrorists' plot?" Julie asked.

"And he probably lost it in the World Trade Center seven years ago before he could hand over the information to the Chinese government." Thompson furthermore explained her theory.

197

"That was the day of 9/11 when the friend of Chris' mother found the locket and gave it to Chris." Max jumped in. "He might have died on that day!"

"If the Chinese spy had information on the terrorist's plot, it would have been information related to the 9/11 attack years ago. What does it have to do with what just happened today?" Christopher could not figure it out.

"Unless it was a plot for a series of multiple attacks…" Julie seemed to be speaking to herself, but the others heard her words.

"That would explain the message inside the locket." Christopher finally agreed.

"In that case, the locket probably held the information on the attack and possibly where the

missing people are being held hostage." Max said hopefully.

Ashley Thompson nodded her head in agreement and added, "The Chinese government had been very worried about terrorist activities in the U.S. spreading to the Olympic site in China. After all, the host country always assumes responsibility for the safety of the athletes and guests attending the Olympic.

"Our police department had learned that the Chinese were very active in the city collecting terrorist information. They even found information that our CIA and FBI did not find.

"We also learned that China planned to use soldiers and police as performers during the Opening and Closing ceremonies for additional protection for

all the world leaders attending the ceremonies." Thompson smiled.

"China used soldiers to perform art?" Max cried with disbelief.

"Too bad I am not serving in the Chinese army! As you know, I love music and art." Thompson grinned while making fun of herself.

They exchanged a good laugh. The children felt more comfortable with Thompson. After some conflicts, they welcomed the discovery that Thompson actually had a sense of humor.

Chapter 21

Boundary of Errors

---

*T*hompson banged her head on the wall.

"That would explain why they so desperately want me to find the locket." She now understood.

She almost made the most unforgivable mistake of handing over the locket to the terrorists, feeling so mad and at herself. She must not be a good

role model for these kids. If anything, they probably looked down at her with disgust.

Julie walked over to put her hand on the officer's shoulder and said gently, "Everyone makes mistakes. The most important thing to correct your mistake is to never repeat it again."

"I lied and made serious errors." Thompson looked at Julie, asking for forgiveness.

"And you regret them now," said Christopher. "My Mom lied too."

"Really?" Julie asked very interestingly, because Christopher never talked anything bad about his mother.

* * * * *

One year Christopher's family was vacationing in Disney World over the Christmas holidays and her mother made a judgment of error and told a lie.

The family always celebrated winter holidays in the city and then went away during the week before the New Year. It was a family tradition as well.

Winter holidays had always been very special to Christopher. He loved Halloween, Thanksgiving, Hanukkah (his dear piano teacher's holiday), Christmas and New Year. While he liked the summer because of the long school break, he loved the winter more because of the holiday atmosphere and family gatherings.

Winter was his favorite season of the year. The air was cool, but people's hearts were warm. He

203

loved sending out holiday cards, putting up holiday decorations, and getting together with friends and family. He looked forward to opening holiday cards from his friends and even enemies.

Last year he wrote a holiday card to a classmate, Jean-Marie, a French boy who had been bullying him in school when Christopher was much younger a few years ago. Christopher wanted to reach out to Jean-Marie, so he spent all night crafting a handmade card. To his own recognition, Christopher's talent was not in craft and art, so the card did not turn out to be as beautiful as he had hoped it to be.

He showed it to Julie and asked Julie for help.

"Julie, what do you think?"

"It's ugly!" Julie did not want to break his heart, but she told the truth.

"I know. I am just not good in art. Can you help me make one?" Christopher tried to recruit her help.

"Then it is not made by you and it won't have the same meaning, Chris.

"You can buy even a better one in a store, but it is not the same as the one you spent all night making.

"You should not hide your strengths and weaknesses from your friend…that is… if you are wishing for a friend."

Julie convinced him. Christopher took her advice and sent the card out with a poem inserted inside and a wish to seal the envelope.

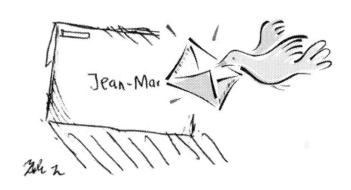

Winter

Out of the air, Summer said,
"This is so boring, I will go to bed,
It is cold and it is dark,
Be careful there is lots of snow and
sleds!"

Out in the North, Santa hears,
Winter shout out sincere,
"Oh Santa, oh Santa, helps the good
girls and boys!"

In the air, some bells start ringing,
A voice comes singing,
and "Ho, ho, ho" is heard,

St. Nick comes out,
he shouts with no doubt,

"Oh the good girls and boys,
Celebrate Winter with great joy!"

Santa dances and prances,
all the way down,
Then "Plop",
he lands on the ground,

He wiggles and squiggles,
dancing around,
All around town,
he hardly makes a sound.

* * * * *

To his surprise, he got a card back from Jean-Marie as well. Jean-Marie thanked him for the "beautiful" card and poem.

The two made up although they still teased each other from time to time and called each other an enemy jokingly.

"That was a small lie you told about my holiday card, Jean-Marie." Christopher said.

"It's not a lie. The poem is beautiful. I wish I could write like you." Jean-Marie responded.

"Sure, but the card is ugly. I can't believe you said it was beautiful." Christopher continued to confront his lie.

"You don't have to lie to make me feel better." Chris assured him.

"Hey, "beautiful" is a subjective word. Have you heard of that phrase 'Beauty is in the eyes of the believers?" Jean-Marie refused to give in.

"Beauty is in the eyes of the beholder!" Christopher corrected him and then they laughed silly.

Winter was definitely his favorite month because winter was magical and filled with warmth and joy like this.

It was a special season also because Christopher's family would go away to a short vacation during the few days before New Year. It was something that Christopher very much looked

forward. He loved to monopolize his parents for a few days, away from home where they were always busy running errands and cuddle up in his parents' hotel bed watching television at night, talking, and laughing.

With too much funs and happiness, people sometimes misbehave. In the case of Christopher's mother, she was a bad girl during the family's visit to Disney World for Christmas holidays.

Christopher started to tell his friends what happened in the Disney trip.

The family was very much looking forward to the famous Disney character dinner at Chef Mickey. It was a dining experience with Disney characters like Mickey, Goofy, and others.

Christopher's mother had tried for weeks to make a reservation at the restaurant without success. The restaurant was fully booked.

Christopher was very disappointed even though he did not say anything. Her mother saw the disappointment hidden in his eyes, so she felt bad.

On the last evening before the end of their trip, there was a big rain storm. His mother figured that many people would not show up for the reservation in the restaurant. She decided to take a chance and drove the family over to Chef Mickey to see if the restaurant had last minute cancellations.

Sure enough, many people did not show up for their reservations and the restaurant had many empty tables, but the restaurant did not have any procedure to reallocate the empty tables even though the guests did not show up.

Christopher's Mom pleaded with the waiters for flexibility to give them one of the empty tables. She made up an excuse.

She asked the waiters to make an exception because it was her son's birthday.

Christopher was astonished that his mother remembered his birthday wrong and corrected her in front of the waiters. She was so embarrassed. She admitted the lie and apologized sheepishly to everyone.

Most importantly, she felt that she had set a bad example for her son. And she regretted that ever since.

Christopher on the other hand benefited from his mother's courage for admitting mistakes. The restaurant wait staff heard the birthday excuse many times from guests before, but never had any kid come forward to point out a parent's mistakes. Never had any parent accepted their child's criticism, admitted their mistakes and apologized to their children in front of the public neither.

The staff laughed for a moment and immediately offered the family one of the empty tables in the restaurant.

Christopher remembered these happy moments but then found himself sad once again.

What happened if he did not find his parents and never saw them again? He wished all these happenings in the last day were simply a dream and started to clutch his head. Sadly, nothing happened. Christopher almost felt angry at himself for not respecting his parents once in a while.

214

His mother told a small lie for him, and he benefited from her embarrassment in public. Although she later explained that it was still a lie no matter how small it was, but did he make the right choice in embarrassing her?

His mother was kind of happy that he uncovered her lie though. She told him that people almost never see their own faults. She said that Christopher made her see the faults in herself and reminded her of errors that she could not see herself even as an adult.

* * * * *

"Everyone makes mistakes, Officer Thompson. My mother made mistakes, too. What's important is to recognize your own mistakes and correct them," Christopher said while putting his hand on Ashley Thompson's shoulder.

"But not every mistake can be corrected. Some mistakes cause consequences that can not be repaired or regretted." Thompson said.

"Agreed. But we are lucky that your error in judgment did not cause irreparable damages yet." Max tried to forgive her.

"You can continue feeling sorry for yourself, or you can choose to help us repair the damages now, if you truly regret what you did." Paul encouraged her, too.

Officer Thompson looked at each of them for support. The kids forgave her. All that she wanted to do now was to repay her debts.

Chapter 22

Quest for Truth

---

*A*shley Thompson felt a jolt of memory as she wondered why they wanted the locket of that Chinese spy.

Why was it dangerous? There must have been a reason. They had already searched the locket well. But what could it have held that was dangerous?

"How are we going to help my family and the others?" Ashley Thompson asked herself.

Why is the fate of her family in the hands of children? She started to cry as she felt hopeless.

"It is useless….

"Even if we find them, it would take another miracle to rescue them," Ashley Thompson said.

Max was not impressed with Thompson's whining and said, "Thompson. You are acting like a baby! You are a police officer. Eventually, all of the bad guys are caught no matter what happens."

Christopher understood Thompson's frustration and asked slowly but firmly, "Tell me, has there ever been a criminal that 100% escaped your clutches?"

Julie added, "Just remember, Officer, do what you think is right…"

Thompson suddenly jumped from her seat, opened the door and ran out of the room. In just a few minutes, she came back with a disk and popped it into the DVD player inside the room.

"It's the Summer Olympic Games Opening Ceremony!" Christopher screamed.

Julie, Max, and Paul went over to Christopher and Thompson and surrounded the TV. They were watching the Olympics opening ceremony for the first time. Because they went away to vacation with their family, they missed watching the spectacle.

"Do you really think that this Olympic opening ceremony has anything to do with the locket?" Julie's question was directed to Christopher and Thompson. She started to feel scared as beads of sweat circled her neck

"This is our only clue so far. We don't have any other," Thompson responded. Christopher nodded in agreement with Thompson for the first time.

Thompson fast forwarded to the segment where the dancers simulated the movements of an ancient printing machine. Sure enough, the Chinese character standing for "harmony" was choreographed by the dancers who were actually soldiers.

Julie was manipulating the locket while watching the ceremony played on the TV. She ran her hand on the symbol over and over again while fixing her eyes on the screen.

Christopher took a glance at her and asked, "What is it, Julie?"

"This segment reminds me of something… in the past… when I was very young." Julie's eyes looked dreamy.

Her words caught Paul's attention. Paul looked up.

"Me too... it seems to be something that I saw when I was very... very young." Paul's voice was a little shaky when he said that.

Paul slowly turned to Julie, locking his thought into Julie's eyes.

"I remember my parents showed me a picture that was taken when I was still an infant. It was taken on their trip to China visiting the Terra Cotta Museum," Paul recalled.

"My birth father was a journalist photographer. My parents took both my twin sibling and I on that working trip to China," said Paul.

Paul took a breath and continued speaking while looking at Julie. "The picture suddenly seemed so vivid after seeing this segment.

"The images of the Great Wall on TV and the dancers, remind me of the terra cotta soldiers standing in the background of the picture that my parents showed me.

"What I remember most was my baby twin sibling in that picture. He was reaching out with his hand to touch the terra cotta soldiers and got stopped by the Chinese police guarding the museum.

"My parents said that he cried hysterically and stopped only when I held his hand to give him comfort." Paul did not stop looking at Julie the whole time he was speaking.

Julie, on the other hand, was completely silent, even though she was locking her sight into Paul's eyes as well.

Julie suddenly turned away from Paul to look at Christopher.

"The Chinese spy must have learned of the terrorist plan. The secret is kept in this locket." She changed the subject unexpectedly, as if she tried to avoid something.

Paul was disappointed that Julie changed the subject. He was looking for a response from Julie to reassure his instinct.

He knew by now that his search for those held hostage by the terrorists may somehow lead to his search for his twin sibling as well, the baby brother, or SISTER perhaps, who was separated from him.

224

He was always thinking of his twin sibling. He had asked his parents many times why they gave away his twin sibling. He asked his stepparents also. None of them told him the reason.

They did not even tell him if his sibling was a boy or girl. His parents simply said it was a mistake they regretted and could not fix.

"Do you understand the message engraved inside this pendant?" Christopher frowned and asked Julie.

He sensed that Julie was avoiding Paul as well. He wanted to find words to comfort Paul, too, but he couldn't. So he just put his hand on Paul's shoulder instead, while waiting for Julie to respond.

"September Repeats....Doomsday...Let Civil kill themselves..." Julie was just repeating the words again and again, allowing flash backs of her memories alternating between the terra cotta soldiers and the terrorist acts of the last day.

The echo that filled the room competed with the music of the opening ceremony on TV.

Christopher, Max and Paul all found themselves repeating the same words while Thompson kept pacing in front of the TV.

Her footsteps became impatient.

The symbol engraved on the cover of the pendant stood for Harmony, while the words engraved inside the cover screamed murder. The words together seemed contradictory and tragic.

What did harmony and an evil plot have to do with one another?

But then what does love have to do with giving up your baby for adoption? Yet, Julie's adopted mother told her that her birth parents gave her up because they loved her, not because they hated her.

Julie wanted to hold on to that belief. Perhaps they were too poor or too ill at the time. Perhaps they could not afford to feed her, so they gave her up so she could have a better life. That's what she would like to believe.

The last thing she wanted to find out would be her parents picking her out from a set of twins to give up for adoption. If they could afford to keep one of the two, why was she not the chosen one?

227

Suddenly Julie no longer wanted to know her birth parents and their reasons for giving her up. Her search for her birth parents would stop today, at least for the time being, because she did not want to know the truth. Her quest for truth is over, she promised herself.

Julie unexpectedly turned to Christopher and asked, "How many people can the Olympic stadium hold?" She knew what was coming up. She braced herself for the answer when she figured out the terrorist evil plot.

Christopher thought for a few seconds and took a guess. "Not sure! I seem to remember the commentator mentioned one hundred thousand.

"Wait...Julie, you don't think...?" Christopher grabbed Julie's hand with such a force that it actually made her feel pain....

Chapter 23

When Birds Abandon the Nest

---

*E*ven though she ordinarily would have howled in pain, this matter was so serious she did not feel a thing.

Julie complained, "What's the matter Chris?"

"The Bird Nest Stadium," Christopher said.

"So? That's the name of the Olympic stadium in China Beijing!" Max screamed in puzzlement.

"Oh My God!" Paul screamed, too.

"Can you kids stop screaming and tell me what's going on?" Thompson could not help whimpering. Her eyes were still very red. "What the heck do you mean by Bird Nest Stadium?"

Christopher took a breath and sat down on a wooden carton next to the old TV.

"When the birds abandon their nest, what happens to the nest?" Christopher hinted.

"I still don't understand Chris. You don't think they put the hostages in China's Bird Nest

Stadium, do you?" Julie said as she sat down on a carton opposite him. "Do you understand it Paul?"

"No, I only said 'Oh my God' because I don't understand him either." Paul flashed as he replied to Julie.

"No. Not in China. The Bird Nest Stadium is only symbolic in the terrorist's plan." Christopher said, but he did not explain further.

He had to think and sort out his thoughts. Flashes of the bubble underneath the subway, the lost pendant, the symbol of harmony, the book of hints, the ancient terra cotta soldiers, and the Olympic Stadium together, merged into a new image. That image resonated in the dream that was shared by the four of them the night before school.

He was going to cling on to that dream, but he suddenly remembered the book of hints. Except for the symbol of harmony, they could not read any other symbols written in the book. The other symbols were not Chinese, but clearly there was something important written.

He needed to know the meaning of the symbols in the book before he could be sure of his instinct.

"The writings in this book are ancient Greek." Christopher suddenly made that statement out of the blue, as he was flipping the pages of the book again.

"Why do you say that?" Thompson asked.

"He is right. The Olympics are an ancient Greek sporting event." Max and Paul both understood.

"And you think the terrorist plan involves using a large sport stadium to hide tens of thousands of people." Julie suddenly understood. She was no less clever than Christopher. She was just distracted by Paul earlier.

"That's not all, Julie. When do you think a bird will abandon its nest?" Christopher asked.

"Only when there is great danger ahead.... or the mother bird will never abandon her young!" Julie answered.

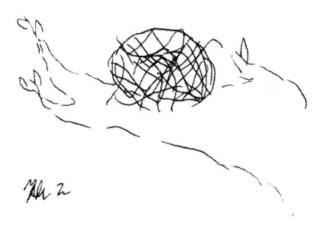

"That's right. When birds abandon their nest, they had to sadly let their young die." Christopher looked at Julie and said each word very slowly and carefully, worrying that he would trigger strong emotion in Julie. After all, Julie was abandoned by her birth parents.

"September Repeats...Doomsday...Let Civil Kill Themselves..." Julie found herself repeating the

words again. She was a strong girl, as Christopher knew. Christopher smiled with satisfaction.

Christopher nodded at her first and then looked at Paul and Max. Both of them nodded their heads. All four of them shared the same thought.

Thompson suddenly jumped up. By now, the kids got used to the police officer's habit of jumping up whenever she was excited. *Did she get trained in police school's line up?* They all thought.

"I am going to tell the FBI to search all sport stadiums in the city." It was Thompson's impulsive reaction, of course.

"Are you sure there is time to search ALL stadiums in the city?" Christopher said with great concern.

"Don't worry! I will get every police and FBI agent to help. I want you to wait here and I'll get a translator to help you read the Greek symbols inside this book. You kids must wait here for me. Don't go anywhere by yourselves." Thompson ordered.

Thompson was actually worried that these crazy kids would start heading to the stadiums on their own. They were brave and smart kids who would do anything to save their families, just like she would. She was not confident that she could keep them safe from taking matters in their own hands.

She actually felt sorry for these kids' parents. *How did they manage to keep these kids out of trouble?* She was thinking to herself.

Chapter 24

The Deadline Revealed

---

*A*s soon as the door closed, the room fell silent.

Finally both Christopher and Julie felt relieved. The silence felt peaceful because hope was in sight. Thompson outlined a plan and took charge of the command. Having an adult taking control made Paul and Max feel protected and safe. They waited patiently inside the room.

Julie looked a bit uncomfortable standing next to Paul. She moved away from him and sat on a chair next to the TV. She took the remote and turned on the volume. They remained quiet, while waiting for Thompson to come back.

Suddenly the door opened! Three FBI agents walked in with a man wearing a dark suit. The children recognized the man. They all got up instantaneously and addressed him.

"Mr. President!" They said.

* * * * *

Officer Thompson walked into the dark room after coming from the police commissioner's office

which was organizing the search plan to begin in a couple hours. The entire city's police force would be involved in this search. She wondered why the interrogation room was so dark. *Where are the kids? Where are the FBI agents and translators? Aren't they supposed to be with the kids here?* She wondered.

The light flashed on and he was pinned to the wall. When she fell down to the floor, she did not see a single soul in the room except for herself. *What is wrong here?* She paused as she stepped over a pamphlet of papers. A piece of paper slowly flied off the door. She staggered to the door and picked up a crushed note. The note said in a red scribbled handwriting: *880 River Ave.* It was written next to some Greek letters. It must have been left behind by the FBI translator.

239

What's this address? The officer was puzzled as she sat down on a stool next to a computer.

The computer was on. Someone was using it before she came in. *It was probably the FBI agents.* She accidentally touched the mouse and the screen showed the GOOGLE page. Someone had searched for 'Yankee Stadium Demolition Date'. Suddenly,

her heart began pounding and her whole body was trembling when she saw the date on the screen.

She immediately jumped out of the room. *880 River Ave.* That's where the kids and the FBI agents had gone. They left her the address because the Yankee Stadium would be demolished in exactly *ONE HOUR!*

Suddenly everything made sense. The hostages were trapped inside Yankee Stadium, which had been abandoned for months waiting for the demolition after the new stadium was built. There were no securities or even lights on site. The helicopter searches earlier could not see anything from the sky.

In one hour, the hostages would be killed and buried, not by any foreigner, but at the hands of their own Americans civilians. The tragedy would take place inside a sports stadium that is the symbol of harmony in the hearts of all American souls!

Running breathlessly in the hallway, Thompson screamed at the top of her lungs to all other police officers.

"Follow me…everyone follow me NOW! This is an order."

The police headquarter was emptied in minutes. FDR was lined up with hundreds of police cars, fire trucks and ambulances racing toward Yankee Stadium on 880 River Ave.

Another dozen helicopters were already circling the sky on top of the stadium, with hundreds of soldiers parachuting into the dark.

Thompson's car had almost approached the stadium when she looked out of the car window. Under the moonlight, she saw the President of the United States, also a former naval aviator, just made a parachute jump from one of the helicopters.

The Commander-in-Chief had joined them in the rescue!

Chapter 25

The Ending Never Written

---

*J*ulie was sitting next to Christopher in the classroom.

Paul and Max were sitting just two rows behind them. This was their first day of school at Hunter. The school finally opened again after the Yankee Stadium near catastrophe.

Most students had already attended the first day of school two weeks ago. Christopher Villson, Julie Herring, Max Fuzzi and Paul Beanstoc never made it to the school two weeks ago for their first day of school. Since then, the school had been closed for two weeks.

The new teacher had asked the class to write an essay about their experience of 'The Big Day ---- First Day of School'. The students were laboring through their paper.

Julie already wrote twenty pages. She has come to the point where she would need to write the ending to her paper.

She glanced at Christopher and quickly learned that he had the same problem. She turned her head back to look at Max and Paul. They gave her a blank look as well.

Quietly, they all put down their pens. They had promised the President that they would not reveal the details of the rescue plan. Moreover, they learned too many secrets that could not be shared with anyone for national security reasons. They could not reveal

the Greeks written in the book, and they could not say a word about a new scientific invention by the Chinese….. or could they?

Coming up next! *Bubbles Gonna Burst!*

Paul tapped on Julie's shoulder gingerly. When she turned back, he handed to her a birthday card and a chocolate kiss. Julie opened the card and found her 'happy birthday poem' inside.

Hershey Kiss

Every night I eat a Hershey kiss

I got a Hershey kiss
And before it reached my mouth
It jumped off my hand
With it's silver top hat
Screaming in the dark garbage can

With a flash light
Crying help, help, help,
So I help him
But by accident the dog reached him
Before I can save him for you

248

Julie opened the silver wrap of the Hershey Kiss. She popped the chocolate into her mouth and carefully slipped the card inside her notebook.

Christopher and Max whispered 'happy birthday' to her. She blushed and gave them a bright smile. Instead of birthday cake, they are going to celebrate with lemon custard pie tonight!

You are invited to visit

BillyChiu.com